In Praise of DOGS

In Praise of DOGS

Compiled by Daniel Farson

Illustrated by Barbara Howes

HARRAP LONDON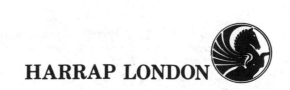

To
Bernard Phillips
Veterinary Surgeon
whose skill and sympathy
is appreciated throughout
North Devon

I am his Highness' dog at Kew;
Pray tell me, sir, whose dog are you?

Inscription on the dog collar presented to
Frederick, Prince of Wales, by Alexander Pope.

First published in Great Britain 1976
by GEORGE G. HARRAP & CO. LTD.
182-184 High Holborn, London WC1V 7AX

© *Daniel Farson 1976*

© *Illustrations Barbara Howes 1976*

ISBN 0 245 53006 1

Composed in VIP Times by Amos Typesetters, Hockley, Essex
and printed and bound in Great Britain
at The Pitman Press, Bath

A dog starv'd at his master's gate
Predicts the ruin of the State.

WILLIAM BLAKE (1757–1827)

Wild Dog crawled into the Cave and laid his head on the Woman's lap, and said: 'O my Friend and Wife of my Friend, I will help your Man to hunt through the day, and at night I will guard your Cave.' . . . .

When the Man waked up he said, 'What is Wild Dog doing here?' And the Woman said, 'His name is not Wild Dog any more, but the First Friend, because he will be our friend for always and always and always.'

RUDYARD KIPLING (1865–1936)
from the *Just So Stories*

Take, however, the first dog you meet with, and the moment he has adopted you for his master, from that moment you are sure of his gratitude and affection. He will love you without calculating what he shall gain by it—his greatest pleasure will be to be near you—and should you be reduced to beg your bread, no poverty will induce him to abandon you. Your friends may, and probably will, do so—the object of your love and attachment will not perhaps like to encounter poverty with you. Your wife by some possibility (it is a rare case, however, if she has received kind treatment) may forget her vows, but your dog will never leave you—he will either die at your feet, or if he should survive you, will accompany you to the grave.

EDWARD JESSE ESQ (1780–1868)
from *Anecdotes of Dogs*

ACKNOWLEDGMENTS

Other Men's Flowers, extract, by Viscount Wavell (1944), reproduced by kind permission of Jonathan Cape Ltd.

Anecdotes of Dogs, by Edward Jesse (Bentley 1846).

The Dog in Health and Disease, by 'Stonehenge' (J. H. Walsh 1879).

The Dogs of the British Islands, by 'Stonehenge' (J. H. Walsh 1886).

'Dog Stories' from *The Spectator* 1895.

A Dog at All Things, by Agnes Lauchlan (Jonathan Cape).

Best Dog Stories, by C. B. Poultney (Faber & Faber 1949).

Best of Dogs, by Eric Parker (Hutchinson 1949).

'Rex', by D. H. Lawrence, first published in *The Dial* (1921) and reproduced here by kind permission of Laurence Pollinger Ltd, and the Estate of the late Frieda Lawrence.

'Memoirs of a Yellow Dog', from *The Four Million,* by O'Henry (Hodder & Stoughton 1906).

Extracts from *Landor: A Replevin,* by Malcolm Elwin (Macdonald 1958), reproduced by kind permission of Eve Elwin.

'Foxl', from *Hitler's Table Talk,* edited by H. R. Trevor-Roper (Weidenfeld & Nicolson 1973).

'Having No Hearts', from *Head in Green Bronze,* by Sir Hugh Walpole, reproduced by kind permission of Sir Rupert Hart-Davis.

Extract reprinted from *Death in the Woods And Other Stories,* by Sherwood Anderson, with the permission of the Liveright Publishing Corporation. Copyright 1933 by Sherwood Anderson. Copyright renewed 1960 by Mrs Eleanor Anderson.

Extract from the *Just So Stories,* by Rudyard Kipling, reproduced by kind permission of Mrs George Bambridge and the Macmillan Company of London and Basingstoke.

Jock of the Bushveld, extracts, by Sir Percy Fitzpatrick (Longmans, Green and Co. Ltd 1907), reproduced by kind permission of the Longman Group Limited.

In The Country, extract, by Kenneth Allsop (Coronet Books 1974), reproduced by kind permission of Betty Allsop.

'Sampy' by John Edwards. First published in the *Daily Mail* and reproduced by kind permission of the author.

'Wully', from *Wild Animals I have Known,* by Ernest Seton-Thompson (later Ernest Thompson Seton). First published by Charles Scribner's Sons, New York, 1898.

'A Crown of Life', extract, from *Tales of Moorland and Estuary,* by Henry Williamson (Panther Books 1970), reproduced by kind permission of the author.

I am indebted to John Dunn who appealed to his listeners in February and March of 1974 on his afternoon programme on BBC Radio 2, for true stories concerning dogs; and to his listeners for their generous response, especially John Jessup whose letter is quoted in full.

My personal thanks to Bob Keating for his helpful advice when I was selecting material.

And to all my dogs for their faithful encouragement.

CONTENTS

The puppy

Littlewood

Once I lived on the bend of the river at Limehouse. My home was above a barge repair yard and I walked back there one summer evening, down Cable Street across the swing bridge over Regent Canal Dock and into Narrow Street. A small boy sat on my doorstep.

'Seen yer pup?'

'I don't have one.'

'You do now.'

Upstairs a group of boys prodded and pushed at some object underneath the sofa, jabbing saucers of milk and bits of bread. Finally they pulled out a lifeless lump of black fur. My housekeeper, Rose, came in from the kitchen. I thought she looked guilty. 'Didn't know what to do for the best,' she said. 'They'd better tell you themselves.' We stared at the mongrel puppy, so young she could barely feed herself.

Two of the boys told me they had bought her in Petticoat Lane the day before, a Sunday. The impulse to part with their money must have been overpowering for they knew that animals were forbidden in the 'Buildings' opposite, where they lived. Sure enough, their father declared he would destroy the dog unless they found a new owner. They looked at me gravely and without much hope.

'Heard you wanted a dog.'

'Yes, a guard dog to scare off burglars, a doberman or alsatian.

Not *this!*' Their eyes stared back so intently I might have been surrounded by a pack of waiting wolves.

'What's she called?' I asked weakly. There was a sigh of relief and their eyes became confident.

'Her name's Trix. Trixie, 'aint it?'

'Oh no it isn't,' I exclaimed, thinking desperately of a suitable feminine name. I had been working all day with Barbara Windsor and Joan Littlewood on a film called *Sparrows Can't Sing*. 'Barbara' sounded silly for a dog, so did 'Joan' for that matter.

'She's going to be called Littlewood,' I declared.

'That's not a dog's name,' said one boy scornfully, 'why call her that?'

'Because of the Pools,' explained Rose, mistakenly but prophetically.

And this is how Littlewood entered my life and became part of it.

When I returned late that night I half expected to find that the dog was dead. Instead, Littlewood leapt into my arms with a cry of relief, fully recovered from the solicitude of small boys.

There is the risk in writing about Littlewood of making her sound too good. She was not a noisy dog, she never yapped, and seldom barked without reason, but neither was she subdued. To say she was obedient might imply an animal capable of cringing, but Littlewood could never do that. It was simply that she accepted me as her companion; Narrow Street as her home; and everyone she met as her friend. She knew no fear because it never occurred to her. She was curious about everything. And skittish.

On my part, I learnt much from Littlewood. I grew to understand the children who brought her in the first place and came to visit her. I explored parts of the East End where I took her for walks, like Greenwich Park with the splendid view over London from the observatory at the top.

She became famous in the East End. She had an alarming desire to explore the world, escaping from the pub I had taken over on the Isle of Dogs, setting out for the docks. She was not dissatisfied; this was a happy wanderlust. Once she was seen bounding down the road towards Blackwall and I flinched, as I hurried after her, at the roar of traffic and the lorries hurtling past. Luckily, two dockers recognized her and brought her back. Another time I was called to collect her from the local police station where I found her tethered to a vast chain, each link larger than herself.

It was a relief to both of us when we left London to live on the

shores of north Devon. My house is beside the sea, with no passing traffic and only the hazards of the countryside such as cliffs and snares and the unnecessary cruelty of barbed wire.

Littlewood took to her new home as if this had always been the object of her wanderlust. She was mesmerized by the sea as if it fulfilled some deep and ancient yearning. She would sit for hours on the stone balcony outside my bedroom, sniffing the breezes blown in from the Atlantic, gazing at Lundy Island on the far horizon.

On the beach she gambolled through the edges of the surf, her feathery tail held high with pleasure. When I swam, she followed me so far out that I had to turn her round and watch her pushed back to the shore by the waves. If someone threw a stick she would hurl herself into the water, however rough, and strike out after it, bringing it back triumphantly.

Littlewood had turned into a black labrador, with a touch of spaniel and the most beautiful, gentle eyes. A mongrel perhaps, but every hair an aristocrat. One day a distinguished man, in a tweed suit, raised his hat and asked: 'Excuse me, but would your little dog be a water dog?' I had never heard of the breed before, but plainly this is what Littlewood would be. It nearly proved her undoing. Lying on the stone when she was wet, even on a low wall below when it was raining, resulted in the damp penetrating her bones and causing arthritis. At one point she was so stiff she had to be carried outside.

Miserable in her inactivity, she was sad to watch. Perhaps it was one of the cures I attempted, or more likely her indomitable stamina, but she recovered. I was careful to rub her down thoroughly now whenever the temptation became too great and she dashed into the sea. She enjoyed this, biting the towel, drying herself by rubbing alongside my bed and then, with a heave, jumping on top of it, wriggling on her back with pleasure. I realized by now that it was either a neat house or one full of dogs. I chose the dogs.

Littlewood's happiness remained undiminished in spite of a series of accidents. Some of these were due to my negligence, like the dreadful night she was locked outside Narrow Street by mistake. I assumed that she was in another room with a friend who was staying the night, but when I woke early in the morning I had a sudden premonition. I found her shivering on the balcony that overlooked the river; there had been a light fall of snow. I wrapped her up and fed her with warmed sugared tea and though she was wretchedly cold she looked up without reproach. Obviously, she was thankful to be home and dry, in every sense. It was I who reproached myself bitterly, especially as an appalling doubt began to overwhelm me. This was confirmed when I crossed to the other side of the house and looked down at the street below; there, on top of the car, were her pawmarks in the snow. She had tried to keep warm from the fading heat of the engine until the early traffic began to thunder past and the workers below found her and carried her through the barge-yard, lifting her on to the balcony. Characteristically, she had not uttered a bark or whine. But when I told my friend what had happened we could not look at each other and I flinch now from the memory.

Another time, in Devon, she was found with such a jagged cut around her eye that it looked as if the eye itself had been destroyed. Just raw, red flesh. I shall never know what happened: a slamming door, a fight with a rat, the dreaded barbed wire? As patient as ever Littlewood drove off with the vet, her damaged face peering out of the window with her indefatigable curiosity.

The stitching by Mr Phillips was more successful than I dared to hope, but Littlewood was so distracted by the irritation that she tried to scratch it free and I would fall asleep, my hands over her paws. The day came at last when Mr Phillips arrived to cut the stitches free and Littlewood stood there in the sunlight, unprotesting as he did so: 'She really is a good old dog,' he said.

Littlewood looked as fine as ever, rather leonine now, her fur bleached by the sun and sea. She was magnificent with old age. Gentle and humorous as ever, but very much the head of her family, deserving and receiving respect. After such a companionship, there was a complete rapport between us. She knew when to leave me alone, knew when to play. It was painful to leave her when I had to travel, and to see her dejection as my suitcases were produced. But this constant grief between dog and owner, the inability to explain that I *would* come back, was compensated by the excitement of my return and such a frantic welcome that I had to calm her. Finally, she would subside with a slight sigh and would even sulk for a moment, a rare weakness but more of a rebuke for my having left her in the first place. And then her tail would start thumping and she would leap up again, unable to suppress her pleasure.

Then, rapidly, she grew too old to walk long distances, though

5

she struggled to do so. One day she stopped in a nearby field and hurried back home, her tail between her legs and such an expression of distress that she might have seen a ghost; perhaps her own? Not gradually, but all too immediately, her limbs seemed to harden and this paralysis spread through her body until Mr Phillips had to be called out early one morning, for the last time. His verdict was inevitable: that if she was allowed to linger she would suffer.

Littlewood *knew*. With one last effort, for even this was difficult now, she licked my hand to reassure me. Her eyes were dimmer, but as generous as ever.

I left the room, and with one huge sob realized our long relationship was over.

It is because of her that this book is compiled, because it was Littlewood who first made me aware of the qualities of the dog as an animal. This is a book about animals rather than pets: the mongrel and the working dog, rather than the pedigree prizewinner. Littlewood was unique, but in this I am praising all dogs for every dog is different. There are stupid dogs and difficult dogs and even dull dogs, but there are less of them than there are of us.

What Littlewood taught me was the dog's *capacity for joy*. From my bedroom window I can look out over the sands in summer and watch many and various dogs at play. It is this scene that makes me like all dogs. And it is their constancy reflected in this book, which makes me admire them.

If I have waxed too sentimental over Littlewood in particular, this is inevitable. She was *my* dog.

Rex

D. H. LAWRENCE
(1885–1930)

All animals, with the exception of the human being, are a pleasure to watch when they are young. The puppy is the most delightful of all.

That sudden, hilarious awareness of life around him. The unfolding mysteries, such as the first sight of a horse — could this be the largest dog in the world? The frantic retreat from the clatter of the first engine. The tantalizing texture of a butterfly or piece of wood. As the butterfly escapes, the wood is chewed simultaneously with a bone, for the day is so crowded that the puppy has not time to concentrate on a single discovery but attempts several manoeuvres at once, with an expression of increasing amazement.

And then, after such ferocious energy, as if the legs can no longer support such activity and have to buckle, the puppy collapses. Stretched on the ground it lies rigid, with eyes tightly closed. Life feigning death.

Even if the boy is dragging the protesting puppy by a lead, the sight is intensely satisfying because the affinity between young dogs and children is *right*. This is part, though only part of the theme of 'Rex'*, by D. H. Lawrence. I never thought of Lawrence writing on such a subject, but it has been one of the pleasures and surprises in preparing this anthology that authors are revealed in a new light. Hugh Walpole, who seemed so remote and sophisticated, is another man when he writes of 'Ugly'. The most unlikely writers are transformed when they describe a dog they have known and loved. Surely Lawrence must have known Rex? For all his genius, he could not have invented him. Was he, too, one of the children who loved him?

Since every family has its black sheep, it almost follows that every man must have a sooty uncle. Lucky if he hasn't two. However, it is only with my mother's brother that we are concerned. She had loved him dearly when he was a little blond boy. When he grew up black, she was always vowing she would never speak to him again. Yet when he put in an appearance, after years of absence, she invariably received him in a festive mood, and was even flirty with him.

He rolled up one day in a dog-cart, when I was a small boy. He was large and bullet-headed and blustering, and this time, sporty. Sometimes he was rather literary, sometimes coloured with business. But this time he was in checks, and was sporty. We viewed him from a distance.

The upshot was, would we rear a pup for him. Now my mother detested animals about the house. She could not bear the mix-up of

* from *'The Mortal Coil and Other Stories'*.

human with animal life. Yet she consented to bring up the pup.

My uncle had taken a large, vulgar public-house in a large and vulgar town. It came to pass that I must fetch the pup. Strange for me, a member of the Band of Hope, to enter the big, noisy, smelly plate-glass and mahogany public-house. It was called The Good Omen. Strange to have my uncle towering over me in the passage, shouting 'Hello, Johnny, what d'yer want?' He didn't know me. Strange to think he was my mother's brother, and that he had his bouts when he read Browning aloud with emotion and éclat.

I was given tea in a narrow, uncomfortable sort of living-room, half kitchen. Curious that such a palatial pub should show such miserable private accommodations, but so it was. There was I, unhappy, and glad to escape with the soft fat pup. It was winter-time, and I wore a big-flapped black overcoat, half cloak. Under the cloak-sleeves I hid the puppy, who trembled. It was Saturday, and the train was crowded, and he whimpered under my coat. I sat in mortal fear of being hauled out for travelling without a dog-ticket. However, we arrived, and my torments were for nothing.

The others were wildly excited over the puppy. He was small and fat and white, with a brown-and-black head: a fox terrier. My father said he had a lemon head — some such mysterious technical phraseology. It wasn't lemon at all, but coloured like a field bee. And he had a black spot at the root of his spine.

It was Saturday night — bath-night. He crawled on the hearth-rug like a fat white teacup, and licked the bare toes that had just been bathed.

'He ought to be called Spot,' said one. But that was too ordinary. It was a great question, what to call him.

'Call him Rex — the King,' said my mother, looking down on the fat, animated little teacup, who was chewing my sister's little toe and making her squeal with joy and tickles. We took the name in all seriousness.

'Rex — the King!' We thought it was just right. Not for years did I realize that it was a sarcasm on my mother's part. She must have wasted some twenty years or more of irony on our incurable naïveté.

It wasn't a successful name, really. Because my father and all the people in the street failed completely to pronounce the monosyllable Rex. They all said Rax. And it always distressed me. It always suggested to me seaweed, and rack-and-ruin. Poor Rex!

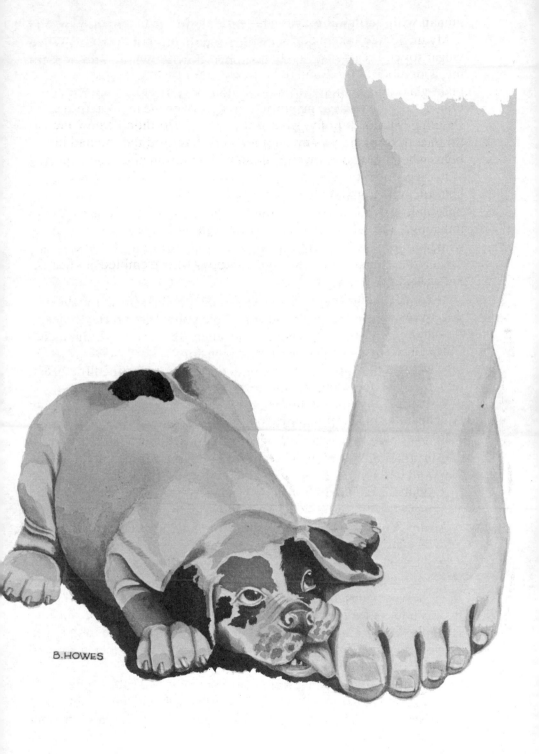

B.HOWES

We loved him dearly. The first night we woke to hear him weeping and whinnying in loneliness at the foot of the stairs. When it could be borne no more, I slipped down for him, and he slept under the sheets.

'I won't have that little beast in the beds. Beds are not for dogs,' declared my mother callously.

'He's as good as we are!' we cried, injured.

'Whether he is or not, he's not going in the beds.'

I think now, my mother scorned us for our lack of pride. We were a little *infra dig,* we children.

The second night, however, Rex wept the same and in the same way was comforted. The third night we heard our father plod downstairs, heard several slaps administered to the yelling, dismayed puppy, and heard the amiable, but to us heartless voice saying 'Shut it then! Shut thy noise, 'st hear? Stop in thy basket, stop there!'

'It's a shame!' we shouted, in muffled rebellion, from the sheets.

'I'll give you shame, if you don't hold your noise and go to sleep,' called our mother from her room. Whereupon we shed angry tears and went to sleep. But there was a tension.

'Such a houseful of idiots would make me detest the little beast, even if he was better than he is,' said my mother.

But as a matter of fact, she did not detest Rexie at all. She only had to pretend to do so, to balance our adoration. And in truth, she did not care for close contact with animals. She was too fastidious. My father, however, would take on a real dog's voice, talking to the puppy: a funny, high, sing-song falsetto which he seemed to produce at the top of his head. ''S a pretty little dog! 's a pretty little doggy! — ay! — yes! — he is, yes! — Wag thy strunt, then! Wag thy strunt, Rexie! — Ha-ha! Nay, tha munna —' This last as the puppy, wild with excitement at the strange falsetto voice, licked my father's nostrils and bit my father's nose with his sharp little teeth.

''E makes blood come,' said my father.

'Serves you right for being so silly with him,' said my mother. It was odd to see her as she watched the man, my father, crouching and talking to the little dog and laughing strangely when the little creature bit his nose and toused his beard. What does a woman think of her husband at such a moment?

My mother amused herself over the names we called him.

'He's an angel — he's a little butterfly — Rexie, my sweet!'

'Sweet! A dirty little object!' interpolated my mother. She and he had a feud from the first. Of course he chewed boots and worried our stockings and swallowed our garters. The moment we took off our stockings he would dart away with one, we after him. Then as he hung, growling vociferously, at one end of the stocking, we at the other, we would cry:

'Look at him, Mother! He'll make holes in it again.' Whereupon my mother darted at him and spanked him sharply.

'Let go, sir, you destructive little fiend.'

But he didn't let go. He began to growl with real rage, and hung on viciously. Mite as he was, he defied her with a manly fury. He did not hate her, nor she him. But they had one long battle with one another.

'I'll teach you, my Jockey! Do you think I'm going to spend my life darning after your destructive little teeth! I'll show you if I will!'

But Rexie only growled more viciously. They both became really angry, while we children expostulated earnestly with both. He would not let her take the stocking from him.

'You should tell him properly, Mother. He won't be driven,' we said.

'I'll drive him farther than he bargains for. I'll drive him out of my sight for ever, that I will,' declared my mother, truly angry. He would put her into a real temper, with his tiny, growling defiance.

'He's sweet! A Rexie, a little Rexie!'

'A filthy little nuisance! Don't think I'll put up with him.'

And to tell the truth, he was dirty at first. How could he be otherwise, so young! But my mother hated him for it. And perhaps this was the real start of their hostility. For he lived in the house with us. He would wrinkle his nose and show his tiny dagger-teeth in fury when he was thwarted, and his growls of real battle-rage against my mother rejoiced us as much as they angered her. But at last she caught him *in flagrante*. She pounced on him, rubbed his nose in the mess, and flung him out into the yard. He yelped with shame and disgust and indignation. I shall never forget the sight of him as he rolled over, then tried to turn his head away from the disgust of his own muzzle, shaking his little snout with a sort of horror, and trying to sneeze it off. My sister gave a yell of despair, and dashed out with a rag and a pan of water, weeping wildly. She sat in the middle of the yard with the befouled puppy, and shedding bitter tears she wiped him and washed him clean. Loudly she reproached my mother. 'Look how much bigger you are than he is. It's a shame, it's a shame!'

'You ridiculous little lunatic, you've undone all the good it would do him, with your soft ways. Why is my life made a curse with animals! Haven't I enough as it is—'

There was a subdued tension afterwards. Rex was a little white chasm between us and our parent.

He became clean. But then another tragedy loomed. He must be docked. His floating puppy-tail must be docked short. This time my father was the enemy. My mother agreed with us that it was an unnecessary cruelty. But my father was adamant. 'The dog'll look a fool all his life, if he's not docked.' And there was no getting away from it. To add to the horror, poor Rex's tail must be *bitten* off. Why bitten? we asked aghast. We were assured that biting was the only way. A man would take the little tail and just nip it through with his teeth, at a certain joint. My father lifted his lips and bared his incisors, to suit the description. We shuddered. But we were in the hands of fate.

Rex was carried away, and a man called Rowbotham bit off the superfluity of his tail in the Nag's Head, for a quart of best and bitter. We lamented our poor diminished puppy, but agreed to find him more manly and *comme il faut*. We should always have been ashamed of his little whip of a tail, if it had not been shortened. My father said it had made a man of him.

Perhaps it had. For now his true nature came out. And his true nature, like so much else, was dual. First he was a fierce, canine little beast, a beast of rapine and blood. He longed to hunt, savagely. He lusted to set his teeth in his prey. It was no joke with him. The old canine Adam stood first in him, the dog with fangs and glaring eyes. He flew at us when we annoyed him. He flew at all intruders, particularly the postman. He was almost a peril to the neighbourhood. But not quite. Because close second in his nature stood that fatal need to love, the *besoin d'aimer* which at last makes an end of liberty. He had a terrible, terrible necessity to love, and this trammelled the native, savage hunting beast which he was. He was torn between two great impulses: the native impulse to hunt and kill, and the strange, secondary, supervening impulse to love and obey. If he had been left to my father and mother, he would have run wild and got himself shot. As it was, he loved us children with a fierce, joyous love. And we loved him.

When we came home from school we would see him standing at the end of the entry, cocking his head wistfully at the open country in front of him, and meditating whether to be off or not: a white, inquiring little figure, with green savage freedom in front of him. A cry from a far distance from one of us, and like a bullet he hurled himself down the road, in a mad game. Seeing him coming, my sister invariably turned and fled, shrieking with delighted terror. And he would leap straight up her back, and bite her and tear her clothes. But it was only an ecstasy of savage love, and she knew it. She didn't care if he tore her pinafores. But my mother did.

My mother was maddened by him. He was a little demon. At the least provocation, he flew. You had only to sweep the floor, and he bristled and sprang at the broom. Nor would he let go. With his scruff erect and his nostrils snorting rage, he would turn up the whites of his eyes at my mother, as she wrestled at the other end of the broom. 'Leave go, sir, leave go!' She wrestled and stamped her foot, and he answered with horrid growls. In the end it was she who had to let go. Then she flew at him, and he flew at her. All the time we had him, he was within a hair's-breadth of savagely biting her. And she knew it. Yet he always kept sufficient self-control.

We children loved his temper. We would drag the bones from his mouth, and put him into such paroxysms of rage that he would twist his head right over and lay it on the ground upside-down, because he didn't know what to do with himself, the savage was so strong in him and he must fly at us. 'He'll fly at your throat one of these days,' said my father. Neither he nor my mother dared have touched Rex's bone. It was enough to see him bristle and roll the whites of his eyes when they came near. How near he must have been to driving his teeth right into us, cannot be told. He was a horrid sight snarling and crouching at us. But we only laughed and rebuked him. And he would whimper in the sheer torment of his need to attack us.

He never did hurt us. He never hurt anybody, though the neighbourhood was terrified of him. But he took to hunting. To my mother's disgust, he would bring large dead bleeding rats and lay them on the hearth-rug, and she had to take them up on a shovel. For he would not remove them. Occasionally he brought a mangled rabbit, and sometimes, alas, fragmentary poultry. We were in terror of prosecution. Once he came home bloody and feathery and rather sheepish-looking. We cleaned him and questioned him and abused him. Next day we heard of six dead ducks. Thank heaven no one had seen him.

But he was disobedient. If he saw a hen he was off, and calling would not bring him back. He was worst of all with my father, who would take him walks on Sunday morning. My mother would not walk a yard with him. Once, walking with my father, he rushed off at some sheep in a field. My father yelled in vain. The dog was at the sheep, and meant business. My father crawled through the hedge, and was upon him in time. And now the man was in a paroxysm of rage. He dragged the little beast into the road and thrashed him with a walking stick.

'Do you know you're thrashing that dog unmercifully?' said a passerby.

'Ay, an' mean to,' shouted my father.

The curious thing was that Rex did not respect my father any the more, for the beatings he had from him. He took much more heed of us children, always.

But he let us down also. One fatal Saturday he disappeared. We hunted and called, but no Rex. We were bathed, and it was bed-time, but we would not go to bed. Instead we sat in a row in our nightdresses on the sofa, and wept without stopping. This drove our mother mad.

'Am I going to put up with it? Am I? And all for that hateful little beast of a dog! He shall go! If he's not gone now, he shall go.'

Our father came in late, looking rather queer, with his hat over his eye. But in his staccato tippled fashion he tried to be consoling.

'Never mind, my duckie, I s'll look for him in the morning.'

Sunday came — oh, such a Sunday. We cried, and didn't eat. We scoured the land, and for the first time realized how empty and wide the earth is, when you're looking for something. My father walked for many miles — all in vain. Sunday dinner, with rhubarb pudding, I remember, and an atmosphere of abject misery that was unbearable.

'Never,' said my mother, 'never shall an animal set foot in this house again, while I live. I knew what it would be! I knew.'

The day wore on, and it was the black gloom of bedtime, when we heard a scratch and an impudent little whine at the door. In trotted Rex, mud-black, disreputable, and impudent. His air of offhand 'How d'ye do!' was indescribable. He trotted around with *suffisance,* wagging his tail as if to say, 'Yes, I've come back. But I didn't need to. I can carry on remarkably well by myself.' Then he walked to his water, and drank noisily and ostentatiously. It was rather a slap in the eye for us.

He disappeared once or twice in this fashion. We never knew where he went. And we began to feel that his heart was not so

14

golden as we had imagined it.

But one fatal day reappeared my uncle and the dog-cart. He whistled to Rex, and Rex trotted up. But when he wanted to examine the lusty, sturdy dog, Rex became suddenly still, then sprang free. Quite jauntily he trotted round — but out of reach of my uncle. He leaped up, licking our faces, and trying to make us play.

'Why, what ha' you done wi' the dog — you've made a fool of him. He's softer than grease. You've ruined him. You've made a damned fool of him,' shouted my uncle.

Rex was captured and hauled off to the dog-cart and tied to the seat. He was in a frenzy. He yelped and shrieked and struggled, and was hit on the head, hard, with the butt-end of my uncle's whip, which only made him struggle more frantically. So we saw him driven away, our beloved Rex, frantically, madly fighting to get to us from the high dog-cart, and being knocked down, while we stood in the street in mute despair.

After which, black tears, and a little wound which is still alive in our hearts.

I saw Rex only once again, when I had to call just once at The Good Omen. He must have heard my voice, for he was upon me in the passage before I knew where I was. And in the instant I knew how he loved us. He really loved us. And in the same instant there was my uncle with a whip, beating and kicking him back, and Rex cowering, bristling, snarling.

My uncle swore many oaths, how we had ruined the dog for ever, made him vicious, spoiled him for showing purposes, and been altogether a pack of mard-soft fools not fit to be trusted with any dog but a gutter-mongrel.

Poor Rex! We heard his temper was incurably vicious, and he had to be shot.

And it was our fault. We had loved him too much, and he had loved us too much. We never had another pet.

It is a strange thing, love. Nothing but love has made the dog lose his wild freedom, to become the servant of man. And this very servility or completeness of love makes him a term of deepest contempt — 'You dog!'

We should not have loved Rex so much, and he should not have loved us. There should have been a measure. We tended, all of us, to overstep the limits of our own natures. He should have stayed outside human limits, we should have stayed outside canine limits.

15

Nothing is more fatal than the disaster of too much love. My uncle was right, we had ruined the dog.

My uncle was a fool, for all that.

Comic dogs

Now here's a funny thing — or not so funny — about comic dog stories. Humorous writers resort to such jocularities as 'dawg' and 'pooch', but this whimsy cannot conceal a cruel streak that suggests an actual dislike of the animal.

Even O'Henry, the most sentimental of raconteurs, deserts his dog at the end of his story 'Ulysses and the Dogman'. Granted, that Ulysses is hardly endearing: 'a vile white dog, loathsomely fat, fiendishly ill-natured, gloatingly intractable towards his despised conductor,' but the Dogman does not sound much fun either. After dragging Ulysses through various swing doors, he is sufficiently fortified with whisky to abandon dog and wife for the prairies and his drinking friend, the ranchman:

> Suddenly the swift landing of three or four heavy kicks was heard, the air was rent by piercing canine shrieks, and a pained, outraged lubberly, bow-legged pudding of a dog ran frenziedly up the street alone.
>
> 'Ticket to Denver,' said Jim.
>
> 'Make it two,' shouted the ex-dogman, reaching for his inside pocket.

Not particularly hilarious, for beast or reader.

L. A. G. Strong not only abandons his dog but tries to poison him in 'A Gift from Christy Keogh':

> Between us we gave him some sort of disinfectant bath, but sure, it was no good. The beagle used to call for him, and sometimes they'd fight like Red Indians all up and down the road, and complaints came pouring in from the neighbours till I thought we'd have to quit. So, in

17

sheer despair, I went out one morning, got arsenic from O'Brien's the chemist, and gave it to the brute in his porridge.

I never saw a dog so much improved as Rover was after that.

F. Anstey, in 'The Black Poodle,' actually shoots the dog, mistaking Bingo for a cat: 'I ran out with the calm pride of a successful revenge to bring in the body of my victim, and I found underneath a laurel, no predatory tom cat, but (as the discerning reader will no doubt have foreseen long since) the quivering carcase of the Colonel's black poodle!'

And all these short stories are supposed to be humorous! The moral is obvious: that dogs are not good subjects for such 'yarns' because, fundamentally, every dog is dignified.

My dog Bonzo is a case in point. She was picked from the litter because she was irrepressibly comic both in looks and personality. She has an alert little face, but it still makes people smile. Her ears grew in the wrong direction when she was a puppy and they perch up oddly even now. There are two or three white hairs on the furthest tip of her tail, and she has white back feet like slippers. By contrast, her front paws resemble white boots. A white ruff and collar are ordinary enough, but the entire effect is heightened by a perfect white nose. From a distance, the nose shines brightly while her dark brown eyes disappear into the blackness of her coat — she is simply nose.

Because she reacts instantly to every noise and movement, people think she is nervous. This would hardly be surprising, with Alice as a mother, especially as Alice was bitten by a snake a few days before Bonzo was born. In fact Bonzo is not nervous, she is hysterical: she screams with delight when she greets the others in the morning; she yells with ecstasy when I put my coat on and a walk is imminent; she shouts with relief when I return home. I have never known a dog talk so much.

Her friend is Streaker and they play together endlessly, racing down to the sands after their breakfast bonio, where they whirl and twirl in circles. Suddenly they stop still, crouch — then off again. There is much stalking through invisible 'high grass'.

Streaker's constant wish is to have a ball thrown for her; when this happens Bonzo sits far back like a small goalie. She has no interest in the ball whatsoever; her role is to seize Streaker by the ruff or the leg after she has retrieved it. This is part of the game and must be by mutual arrangement, otherwise Streaker would find this growling, hanging object exasperating. And it must be a sense of loyalty that makes Bonzo so vigilant, for she never seems to enjoy the game that much. Her toy is an avocado pear stone which she tosses into the air.

In the evenings, when the others are locked up, Bonzo and Streaker play on the sofa emulating tigers. They know just how far to go: Streaker snapping her powerful jaws ferociously, Bonzo darting out of reach, then that sudden rigid silence as if frozen, and she leaps back again.

They are perfect opposites: Streaker, large, amiable and slightly foolish; Bonzo, small and sharp. They are devoted. Bonzo may appear timid, but when Blacky was trying to intimidate Streaker, Bonzo tore into her with such tenacity that there has been no trouble since.

There are moments when Bonzo seems mystified by so much happiness, almost worried as if bad news must be waiting round the corner. When we go to the estuary of the Taw and Torridge rivers, to collect mussels, I encourage her to join the others as they walk along the sands to fish, because the sharp-edged shells might cut into her paws, but after a while she comes bounding back to make certain I am still there. Once, when the shells did hurt her, she sat on a distant sandbank and howled with such anguish that I hurried back. And off she bounded again to make certain the others were all right.

Because she has grown up beside me, I can recognize these shades of character, and when we are alone I praise her with the utmost gravity in case she needs reassurance. At such moments she is still, with a sidelong look, all white of eye. I can recognize glimpses of that sympathy which blessed her great grandmother, Littlewood.

So I am startled when others still think of her as a comic: like the boy who exclaimed so offensively: 'That dog looks more like a cat!' I was astonished when a friend remarked: 'You could never call her a pretty dog, could you?'

I looked at him and realized he was serious; then I looked at Bonzo. That delightful face smiled back at me. How odd of my friend, that he should fail to see her infinite beauty.

Never treat your dog as a comic. This is as condescending as baby talk, which leads me into the next story 'Memoirs of a Yellow Dog', which must seem a curious choice after my earlier criticism of O'Henry. But this story shows both dog and dogman, and the author, in a happier light.

Memoirs of a yellow dog

O'HENRY

(1862–1910)

I don't suppose it will knock any of you people off your perch to read a contribution from an animal. Mr Kipling and a good many others have demonstrated the fact that animals can express themselves in remunerative English, and no magazine goes to press nowadays without an animal story in it, except the old-style monthlies that are still running pictures of Bryan and the Mont Pelée horror.

But you needn't look for any stuck-up literature in my piece, such as Bearoo, the bear, and Snakoo, the snake, and Tammanoo, the tiger, talk in the jungle books. A yellow dog that's spent most of his life in a cheap New York flat, sleeping in a corner on an old sateen underskirt (the one she spilled port wine on at the Lady Longshoremen's banquet), mustn't be expected to perform any tricks with the art of speech.

I was born a yellow pup; date, locality, pedigree and weight unknown. The first thing I can recollect, an old woman had me in a basket at Broadway and Twenty-third trying to sell me to a fat lady. Old Mother Hubbard was boosting me to beat the band as a genuine Pomeranian - Hambletonian - Red - Irish - Cochin - China Stoke - Pogis fox terrier. The fat lady chased a V around among the samples of gros grain flannelette in her shopping bag till she cornered it, and gave up. From that moment I was a pet — a mamma's own wootsey squidlums. Say, gentle reader, did you ever have a 200-pound woman breathing a flavour of Camembert cheese and Peau d'Espagne pick you up and wallop her nose all over you, remarking all the time in an Emma Eames tone of voice: 'Oh, oo's um oodlum, doodlum, woodlum, toodlum, bitsy-witsy skoodlums?'

From a pedigreed yellow pup I grew up to be an anonymous yellow cur looking like a cross between an Angora cat and a box of lemons. But my mistress never tumbled. She thought that the two primeval pups that Noah chased into the ark were but a collateral branch of my ancestors. It took two policemen to keep her from entering me at the Madison Square Garden for the Siberian bloodhound prize.

I'll tell you about that flat. The house was the ordinary thing in New York, paved with Parian marble in the entrance hall and cobblestones above the first floor. Our flat was three fl—well, not flights—climbs up. My mistress rented it unfurnished, and put in the regular things — 1903 antique upholstered parlour set, oil chromo of geishas in a Harlem tea house, rubber plant and husband.

By Sirius! there was a biped I felt sorry for. He was a little man with sandy hair and whiskers a good deal like mine. Henpecked? — well, toucans and flamingoes and pelicans all had their bills in him. He wiped the dishes and listened to my mistress tell about the cheap, ragged things the lady with the squirrel-skin coat on the second floor hung out on her line to dry. And every evening while she was getting supper she made him take me out on the end of a string for a walk.

If men knew how women pass the time when they are alone they'd never marry. Laura Lean Jibbey, peanut brittle, a little almond cream on the neck muscles, dishes unwashed, half an hour's talk with the iceman, reading a package of old letters, a couple of pickles and two bottles of malt extract, one hour peeking through a hole in the window shade into the flat across the air-shaft — that's about all there is to it. Twenty minutes before time for him to come home from work she straightens up the house, fixes her rat so it won't show, and gets out a lot of sewing for a ten-minute bluff.

I led a dog's life in that flat. 'Most all day I lay there in my corner watching the fat woman kill time. I slept sometimes and had pipe dreams about being out chasing cats into basements and growling at old ladies with black mittens, as a dog was intended to do. Then she would pounce upon me with a lot of that drivelling poodle palaver and kiss me on the nose — but what could I do? A dog can't chew cloves.

I began to feel sorry for Hubby, dog my cats if I didn't. We looked so much alike that people noticed it when we went out; so we shook the streets that Morgan's cab drives down, and took to climbing the piles of last December's snow on the streets where cheap people live.

One evening when we were thus promenading, and I was trying to look like a prize St. Bernard, and the old man was trying to look like he wouldn't have murdered the first organ-grinder he heard play Mendelssohn's wedding-march, I looked up at him and said, in my way:

'What are you looking so sour about, you oakum trimmed lobster? She don't kiss you. You don't have to sit on her lap and listen to talk that would make the book of a musical comedy sound like the maxims of Epictetus. You ought to be thankful you're not a dog. Brace up, Benedick, and bid the blues begone.'

The matrimonial mishap looked down at me with almost canine intelligence in his face.

'Why, doggie,' says he, 'good doggie. You almost look like you could speak. What is it, doggie — Cats?'

Cats! Could speak!

But, of course, he couldn't understand. Humans were denied the speech of animals. The only common ground of communication upon which dogs and men can get together is in fiction.

In the flat across the hall from us lived a lady with a black-and-tan terrier. Her husband strung it and took it out every evening, but he always came home cheerful and whistling. One day I touched noses with the black-and-tan in the hall, and I struck him for an elucidation.

'See, here, Wiggle-and-Skip', I says, 'you know that it ain't the nature of a real man to play dry nurse to a dog in public. I never saw one leashed to a bow-wow yet that didn't look like he'd like to lick every other man that looked at him. But your boss comes in every day as perky and set up as an amateur prestidigitator doing the egg trick. How does he do it? Don't tell me he likes it.'

'Him?' says the black-and-tan. 'Why, he uses Nature's Own Remedy. He gets spifflicated. At first when we go out he's as shy as the man on the steamer who would rather play pedro when they make 'em all jackpots. By the time we've been in eight saloons he don't care whether the thing on the end of his line is a dog or a catfish. I've lost two inches of my tail trying to sidestep those swinging doors.'

The pointer I got from that terrier — vaudeville please copy — set me to thinking.

One evening about six o'clock my mistress ordered him to get busy and do the ozone act for Lovey. I have concealed it until now, but that is what she called me: The black-and-tan was called 'Tweetness.' I consider that I have the bulge on him as far as you could chase a rabbit. Still 'Lovey' is something of a nomenclatural tin can on the tail of one's self-respect.

At a quiet place on a safe street I tightened the line of my custodian in front of an attractive, refined saloon. I made a dead-ahead scramble for the doors, whining like a dog in the press despatches that lets the family know that little Alice is bogged while gathering lilies in the brook.

'Why, darn my eye if the saffron-coloured son of a seltzer lemonade ain't asking me in to take a drink. Lemme see — how long's it been since I saved shoe leather by keeping one foot on the foot-rest? I believe I'll ——'

I knew I had him. Hot Scotches he took, sitting at a table. For an hour he kept the Campbells coming. I sat by his side rapping for the waiter with my tail, and eating free lunch such as mamma in her flat never equalled with her homemade truck bought at a delicatessen store eight minutes before papa comes home.

When the products of Scotland were all exhausted except the rye bread the old man unwound me from the table leg and played me outside like a fisherman plays a salmon. Out there he took off my collar and threw it into the street.

'Poor doggie,' says he; 'good doggie. She shan't kiss you any more. 'S a darned shame. Good doggie, go away and get run over by a street car and be happy.'

I refused to leave. I leaped and frisked around the old man's legs happy as a pug on a rug.

'You old flea-headed woodchuck-chaser,' I said to him — 'you moon-baying, rabbit-pointing, egg-stealing old beagle, can't you see that I don't want to leave you? Can't you see that we're both Pups in the Wood and the missis is the cruel uncle after you with the dish towel and me with the flea liniment and a pink bow to tie on my tail. Why not cut that all out and be pards for evermore?'

Maybe you'll say he didn't understand — maybe he didn't. But he kind of got a grip on the Hot Scotches, and stood still for a minute, thinking.

'Doggie,' says he finally, 'we don't live more than a dozen lives on this earth, and very few of us live to be more than 300. If I ever see that flat any more I'm a flat, and if you do you're flatter; and that's no flattery. I'm offering 60 to 1 that Westward Ho wins out by the length of a dachshund.'

There was no string, but I frolicked along with my master to the Twenty-third Street ferry. And the cats on the route saw reason to give thanks that prehensile claws had been given them.

On the Jersey side my master said to a stranger who stood eating a currant bun:

'Me and my doggie, we are bound for the Rocky Mountains.'

But what pleased me most was when my old man pulled both of my ears until I howled, and said:

23

'You common, monkey-headed, rat-tailed, sulphur-coloured son of a door mat, do you know what I'm going to call you?'

I thought of 'Lovey,' and I whined dolefully.

'I'm going to call you "Pete",' says my master; and if I'd had five tails I couldn't have done enough wagging to do justice to the occasion.

The sagacity of dogs

'Dogs, sir?'

'Not just now,' said Mr Winkle.

'Ah! you should keep dogs — fine animals — sagacious creatures — dog of my own once — pointer — surprising instinct — out shooting one day — entering enclosure — whistled — dog stopped — whistled again — Ponto — no go; stock still — called him — Ponto, Ponto — wouldn't move — dog transfixed — staring at a board — looked up, saw an inscription — "Gamekeeper has orders to shoot all dogs found in this enclosure" — wouldn't pass it — wonderful dog — valuable dog that — very.'

'Singular circumstance that,' said Mr Pickwick. 'Will you allow me to make a note of it?'

'Certainly, sir, certainly — hundred more anecdotes of the same animal.'

CHARLES DICKENS *(1812–70)*

From *The Pickwick Papers*

'Sagacious creatures,' said Mr Jingle. 'Sagacity' is the perfect word, implying discernment rather than knowledge. There are many instances of sagacity which have nothing to do with 'tricks', and there are few sights so odious as dancing dogs in frills. Even when a performing dog is an essential part of his master's Act — like a Punch and Judy on the sands — this is only slightly more acceptable. In Southend after the First World War, a dog worked in a promenade side show, tapping out the answers with his paw while his master wrote the questions on a blackboard, selecting different coloured handkerchiefs, and the like. The letter-writer, T. Ball, (one of the listeners who responded generously to the appeal for information made on my behalf by John Dunn during

25

his afternoon programmes on BBC Radio 2 in February and March 1974) wrote of this show: 'The show owner was an oldish man and referred in his spiel to many years' performance with successive dogs of the same family on the same pitch. I judge the show had started well before the turn of the century and had, when I saw it, a melancholy perfection which evoked pity for the animal as well as admiration for the trainer.' That last phrase sums it up. Dogs hate being laughed *at,* and are far too dignified to make mockery of *us.*

Another correspondent, John Jessup, gives a typical example of a dog's sagacity in helping his owners:

'My Christmas present four years ago from my wife was a fine yellow labrador puppy whom we called Marcus. We were living in Shepperton at the time and when he was about six months old I started taking Marcus to obedience classes. He is a beautiful and intelligent dog but has always preferred to do what he wants — i.e., he is stubborn! We had a young daughter about eight months old and were being pressed to accept an invitation to dinner with some close relatives. We had to cancel this on two previous occasions and were now all set for making it "third time lucky". Our babysitter was a very pleasant lady in her sixties and, as it turned out, this was the first and last time she babysat for us. When she arrived on the fateful evening we did the usual things like showing her how the television worked, but she asked, as it was a beautiful June evening, if she could look at our garden.

'We left for the most expensive restaurant about six miles away and were about to start a most sumptuous first course when the bandleader came to the microphone and said there was a telephone call for Mrs Jessup. I decided not to start my meal and joined my wife at the phone to hear her say: "What — an ambulance has been called? We will be right back."

'I drove like a maniac back to our home learning from my distressed wife that it was a garbled message from a complete stranger who said, not to worry, the ambulance had been called. We arrived home and sure enough there was the ambulance — blue light flashing — outside our house.

'At our front gate was a stretcher onto which the babysitter, with a badly broken ankle, was being lifted.

'What had happened was this. Our sprinkler had been on in our garden and I suppose the soles of the babysitter's leather shoes had become damp and as she descended the steps on to our patio she

slipped and broke her ankle.

She then dragged herself through the house, with Marcus licking her face and very concerned, until she came to our front door. As soon as she opened it, Marcus disappeared, jumping over the front gate and running off down the road.

'A few moments later a couple arrived at the front gate with Marcus tugging at the man's trousers. Apparently, they had been walking approximately 200 yards down the road when Marcus ran up to the man and grabbed hold of his trousers in his teeth and started to drag the man in the direction of our house.

'The man naturally thought that he was being assaulted but his wife said: "I think the dog is trying to tell you something."

'It was that man who telephoned the restaurant. When the babysitter said she was very worried about the baby, he went upstairs to our daughter's room only to be met by a ferocious Marcus who was guarding the door and wouldn't let anyone pass. This was where he was when I went upstairs.

'The ward at the hospital, where they took the babysitter, was full of "Marcus the hero dog", but they didn't know that he soon reverted to his amiable stubbornness and has remained thus to this very day.'

Many similar instances have been recorded: Edward Jesse tells of a shepherd who lost his child and his dog when a sudden mist descended on the mountains:

'Next morning by day-break, the shepherd, accompanied by a band of his neighbours, set out in search of the child, but, after a day spent in fruitless fatigue, he was at last compelled, by the approach of night, to descend from the mountain. On returning to his cottage he found that the dog, which he had lost the day before, had been home, and, on receiving a piece of cake, had instantly gone again. For several successive days the shepherd renewed the search for his child, but still, on returning at evening disappointed to his cottage, he found that the dog had been home, and, on receiving his usual allowance of cake, had instantly disappeared. Struck with this circumstance he remained at home one day, and when the dog, as usual, departed with his piece of cake, he resolved to follow him, and find out the cause of his strange procedure. The dog led the way to a cataract, at some distance from the spot where the shepherd had left his child. The banks of the cataract almost joined at the top, yet separated by an abyss of immense depth; presenting that appearance which so often astonishes and appals travellers who frequent the Grampian Mountains, and indicates that these stupendous chasms were not the silent work of time, but the sudden effect of some violent convulsion of the earth. Down one of these rugged and almost perpendicular descents, the dog began, without hesitation, to make his way, and at last disappeared into a cave, the mouth of which was almost on a level with the torrent. The shepherd with some difficulty followed, but, upon entering the cave, what were his emotions when he beheld his lost child eating with much satisfaction the cake, which the dog had just brought to him, while the faithful animal stood by, eyeing his young charge with the utmost complacence?

'From the situation in which the child was found, it appears that he had wandered to the brink of the precipice and then either fallen or scrambled down till he reached the cave, which the dread of the torrent had probably prevented him from quitting. The dog had traced him to the spot, and afterwards prevented him from starving by giving up to him the whole, or the greater part, of his own daily allowance. He appears never to have quitted the child by night or day, except when it was necessary to go for food, and then he was always seen running at full speed to and from the cottage.'

Quoted from the *Monthly Magazine* 1802.

'The dog to the rescue' is a constant theme. In a museum in Naples there is a Roman bronze showing two large dogs 'dragging from the sea some apparently drowned persons'. These were forerunners of the Newfoundland dog, the Saint Bernard of the sea though less well known than that famous breed kept near the peak of Mount Bernard for rescuing lost travellers from the snow.

In France, Newfoundland dogs were trained and kept on the banks of the Seine as 'a sort of Humane Society Corps. By throwing the stuffed figure of a man into a river, and requiring the dog to fetch it out, he is soon taught to do so when necessary, and thus he is able to rescue drowning persons.' Edward Jesse adds that 'The delight of the Newfoundland Dog appears to be in the preservation of the lives of the human race,' and quotes this instance:

'A vessel was driven by a storm on the beach of Lydd, in Kent. The surf was rolling furiously. Eight men were calling for help, but not a boat could be got off for their assistance. At length a gentleman came on the beach accompanied by his Newfoundland dog. He directed the attention of the noble animal to the vessel, and put a short stick into his mouth. The intelligent and courageous dog at once understood his meaning, and sprung into the sea, fighting his way through the foaming waves. He could not, however get close enough to the vessel to deliver that with which he was charged, but the crew joyfully made fast a rope to another piece of wood and threw it towards him. The sagacious dog saw the whole business in an instant — he dropped his own piece, and immediately seized that which had been cast to him; and then, with a degree of strength and determination almost incredible, he dragged it through the surge and delivered it to his master. By this means, a line of communication was formed, and every man on board saved.

The Newfoundland dog was also a messenger and faithful watchdog: 'A sailor attended by a Newfoundland dog, became so intoxicated that he fell on the pavement in Piccadilly, and was unable to rise, and soon fell asleep. The faithful dog took a position at his master's head, and resisted every attempt made to remove him. The man, having at last slept off the fumes of his intoxicating libations, awoke, and being told of the care his dog had taken of him, exclaimed — "this is not the first time he has kept watch over me".'

Jesse gives another example showing the dog's loyalty unto death:

'A chimney sweeper had ordered his dog, a half-bred mastiff, to lie down on his soot bag, which he had placed inadvertently almost in the middle of a narrow back street in the town of Southampton. A loaded coal-cart passing by, the driver desired the dog to move out of the way. On refusing to do so, he was scolded, then beaten, first gently, and afterwards with a smart application of the cart-whip, but all to no purpose. The fellow, with an oath, threatened to drive over the dog, and he did so, the faithful animal endeavouring to arrest the progress of the wheel by biting it. He thus allowed himself to be killed sooner than abandon his trust.'

There have been cases, even, of a dog who will stand guard over a consignment of food, and starve to death rather than break into it.

The homing instinct

Too many cases of the homing instinct in the dog have been recorded to dismiss this as coincidence. Sometimes the dog has been removed to unfamiliar, alien territory — other times he has been left behind and crosses countryside he has never seen before — and there is no logical explanation whatsoever.

There is one case that fascinates me, recorded in *The Spectator* on 8th June 1895. A Chairman of the Bench of Magistrates in the West Country was the authority: a farmer was the tenant of one of his estates near the River Severn and possessed a favourite dog, who slept at the foot of his bed every night. But when his brother emigrated to Canada, the farmer gave him the dog as a travelling companion and learnt later that they had arrived safely at a farm in the interior, several days' journey from the point where they landed. A second letter followed to say the dog had disappeared. Surprisingly, soon after that the dog returned.

'Inquiries were made, and the dog's course was traced backwards to the River Severn, thence to Bristol, and thence to a port in Canada. It appeared that, after running from his home in Canada to the seaport, he selected there a vessel bound for Bristol, and shipped on board. After arriving at the Bristol basin, he found out a local vessel trading up and down the River Severn and transferred himself to her deck. When he reached the neighbourhood of Gloucester, the dog must have jumped into the Severn and reached the shore nearest to his old home.'

This journey would seem incredible, except that so many similar instances have been documented.

Can there be an element of telepathy which directs the animal, even though he has been forsaken by his master? Dogs have drawn the attention of passengers in a train, in order to jump out at the right station. Lost in a foreign town, they have walked directly through strange, crowded streets to some point of recognition. It would be tempting to think that the prevalence of such stories in the past was partly explained by a less urban community with no distracting fumes or fear of passing cars, but another astonishing journey was recorded in the Press as recently as 30th December 1973.

Judging by the photographs, Barry was a splendid alsatian and the constant companion of a young man in West Germany called

Armin de Broi, but after five years the landlord of their flat complained that Barry had grown too large and would have to leave. Reluctantly, the de Broi family sold the dog to an Italian who was returning to his home in southern Italy. Within a short time Barry escaped and started his epic walk home. It took fifteen months and he travelled 1 200 miles from Bari at the toe of Italy to Solingen in the Ruhr, and was found whimpering at the door of his old flat on Christmas Eve 1973. Utterly exhausted and footsore, he was nursed back to health by the family — but the landlord's rule was enforced again. This time there was no betrayal.

'We'd rather move than let him go again,' said Armin de Broi. 'We could never repay his loyalty with such cruelty.' A happy ending to an act of triumphant endurance.

Whatever the explanation, such incidents are glorious proof that the dog retains the instinct of the untamed animal: as miraculous as the migrating bird that flies to Africa or the salmon that returns from the ocean to the river where it was spawned.

But of course there is no reason why dogs should not possess senses unknown to us; indeed it would be surprising if they did not. When one of my dogs was run over several hundred miles away, the others who were with me in Devon reacted *exactly* as if they knew. For no apparent reason their usual cheerfulness was replaced by a disturbed wretchedness. In this case it is possible that the telepathy came from *me,* for I had been told of the news by phone, but when John Dunn kindly asked listeners to his afternoon programme on BBC Radio 2, as mentioned previously, to send in stories relating to dogs, he forwarded these replies among many others. One lady wrote:

> We had an Elkhound who was devoted to my father. When I was ten, my father, mother, sister (who was ten years older) and I went to the Lakes for our Easter holiday leaving the dog with my sister's fiancé. On Easter Monday my father was taken ill with pneumonia and four nights later my sister's fiancé was sitting reading with the dog at his feet when suddenly she sat up trembling all over and then put up her head and howled and howled. The following morning he got a telegram saying my father had died at 8.30 the night before. Have dogs a sense which can travel ninety odd miles?

Another letter described

> Lassie and her pup Domino: Lassie was a real character; Domino was the runt of the litter, a very earnest and loyal little fellow completely devoted to his Mum. When Lassie died, Domino was twenty-five miles

away living with my parents. Domino got up from where he had been lying, lifted up his head and howled as though his little heart would break. My father guessed immediately that something was wrong and phoned me to find out what had happened. Domino is now twelve years old and has never howled either before or since that event.

Companionship

We are alone, absolutely alone, on this planet; and, amid all the forms of life that surround us, not one, excepting the dog, has made an alliance with us.
MAURICE MAETERLINCK
from *My Dog*

Anecdotes of dogs

(an extract)
EDWARD JESSE

A French writer has boldly affirmed that with the exception of women, there is nothing on earth so agreeable, or so necessary to the comfort of man, as the dog. This assertion may readily be disputed, but still it will be allowed that man, deprived of the companionship and services of the dog, would be a solitary and, in many respects, a helpless being. Let us look at the shepherd, as the evening closes in and his flock is dispersed over the almost inaccessible heights of mountains; they are speedily collected by his indefatigable dog — nor do his services end here, he guards either the flock, or his master's cottage by night, and a slight caress, and the coarsest food, satisfy him for all his trouble. The dog performs the services of a horse in the more northern regions, while in Cuba and some other hot countries, he has been the scourge and terror of runaway negroes.

In the destruction of wild beasts, or the less dangerous stag, or in attacking the bull, the dog has proved himself to possess pre-eminent courage. In many instances he has died in the defence of his master. He has saved him from drowning, warned him of approaching danger, served him faithfully in poverty and distress, and if deprived of sight, has gently led him about. When spoken to, he tried to hold conversation with him by the movement of his tail, or the expression of his eyes. If his master wants amusement in the field or wood, he is delighted to have an opportunity of procuring it for him; if he finds himself in solitude, his dog will be a cheerful and agreeable companion, and may be, when death comes, the last to forsake the grave of his beloved master.

'Camp'

Sir Walter Scott's favourite dog Camp, a bull terrier, described in the reminiscences of John Gibson Lockhart, his son-in-law.

1805: He was very handsome, very intelligent, and naturally very fierce, but gentle as a lamb among the children. As for the more locomotive Douglas and Percy (they were 'large' dogs and youthful) he kept one window of his study open, whatever might be the state of the weather, that they might leap out and in as the fancy moved them. He always talked to Camp as if he understood what was said and the animal certainly did understand not a little of it; in particular, it seemed as if he perfectly comprehended on all occasions that his master considered him as a sensible and steady friend, the greyhounds as volatile young creatures whose freaks must be borne with.

1809: . . . became incapable of accompanying Scott on his rides; but he preserved his affection and sagacity to the last. At Ashestiel, as the servant was laying the cloth for dinner, he would address the dog lying on his mat before the fire, and say, 'Camp, my good fellow, the Sheriff's coming home by the ford — or by the hill'; and the sick animal would immediately bestir himself to welcome his master, going out at the back door or the front door, according to the direction given, and advancing as far as he was able, either towards the ford of the Tweed, or the bridge over the Glenkinnon burn beyond Laird Nippy's gate. He died about January 1809, and was buried in a fine moonlight night, in the little garden behind the house in Castle Street, immediately opposite to the window at which Scott usually sat writing. My wife tells me she remembers the whole family standing in tears about the grave, as her father himself smoothed down the turf above Camp with saddest expression of face she had ever seen in him. He had been engaged to dine abroad that day, but apologised on account of 'the death of a dear old friend'.

'A blessing' of dogs

Walter Savage Landor (1775–1864) — the very name of the writer suggests a harshness—and so I imagined him until I read the distinguished biography by my friend and neighbour, the late Malcolm Elwin.* He recorded Landor's delightful affinity with dogs:

> His allowance to animals of natural intelligence and a capacity for feeling comparable with humans was seen by Dickens only as an eccentricity fit for caricature in Boythorn's canary. Few men of his time loved and understood animals so well, and his devotion to dogs equalled that of Galsworthy, who has written more vividly of canine character than any other writer. 'Dogs,' said Landor, 'are blessings, true blessings.'

It was not until late middle age that he came to love dogs of his own. He was fifty-five when he met Parigi in 1830, writing to his sister with the exciting news: 'I have bought a shepherd dog, with a tail that curls over the back, and upright ears. These ears look stiff, but they are more pliable than any others. The back is yellowish, the rest whitish, the nose very pointed, and the teeth so sharp, that these dogs are called here wolf dogs, *Cani lupi*.' At that time Landor was living in Italy. Elwin relates: 'He would take Parigi's head between his knees, and say, "Ah, if Lord Grey (or any other notoriety of the hour) had a thousandth part of your sense how different would be things in England".'

He despised people who were afraid of dogs: 'When a dog flies at you, reason with it and remember how well behaved the Molossian dogs were when Ulysses sat down in the midst of them as an equal.'

He could not understand people who disliked dogs: 'Someone told me that your illustrious friend Goethe hates dogs. God forgive him, if he did. I can never believe it of him. They too are half-poets; they are dreamers. Do any other animals dream? For my part, as you know, I love them heartily. They are grateful, they are brave, they are communicative, and they never play at cards.'

Back in England, now in his old age, he received a white pomeranian from his daughter. The dog became known as Pomero. Elwin writes that 'he found the lonely man's more than human companionship in his dog' and this is confirmed in a letter during one of Landor's absences from home:

Landor: A Raplevin. Malcolm Elwin (Macdonald 1958).

Daily do I think of Bath and Pomero. I fancy him lying on the narrow window sill, and watching the good people go to church. He has not yet made up his mind between the Anglican and Roman Catholic; but I hope he will continue in the faith of his forefathers, if it will make him happier.

As always, the absence was forgotten in the happiness of the return:

His joy at seeing me amounted to madness. His bark was a scream of delight. He is now sitting on my head, superintending all I write, and telling me to give his love.

When someone asked if he was prepared to sell the dog, Landor exclaimed: 'Not for a million of money . . . a million would not make me at all happier, and the loss of Pomero would make me miserable for life.'

But, of course, such a loss was inevitable. Pomero died in 1856, when Landor was eighty-one. Landor wrote to his friend John Forster:

Everybody in this house grieves for Pomero; the cat lies day and night upon his grave; and I will not disturb the kind creature, though I want to plant some violets upon it, and to have his epitaph placed around his little urn.

Malcolm Elwin records the old man's grief: 'The dog was his inseparable companion, trotting at his heels on his walks, lying at his feet as he sat in the park and barking at the passers-by, encouraged in noisiness by his master's boisterous manner of playing with him. When Pomero failed to return with him from a walk, Landor would refuse to eat his dinner and would stamp about the room, raving that the dog was murdered, kidnapped, or pelted with stones, that he would go out to scour the city for him, that he would give a hundred pounds — even his whole fortune to anyone who brought him back alive.' Now, the silence in his room seemed like a reproach and 'the sight of the old man himself in his loneliness, sitting so still and quiet in his armchair, without even the distraction of his noisy little friend, was infinitely pathetic'.

Yet there was one further companion, Giallo, another pomeranian who joined him in Florence two years later. When he was asked if he thought that dogs went to heaven, Landor replied: 'Why not? They have all the good and none of the bad qualities of man.' But he knew that *he* was not to experience the grief of his dog's death this time:

> Giallo! I shall not see thee dead,
> Nor raise a stone above thy head,
> For I shall go some years before,
> Where thou will leap at me no more,
> Nor bark, as now, to make me mind,
> Asking me, am I deaf or blind:
> No Giallo, but I shall be soon:
> And thou wilt scratch my turf and moan.

Landor wrote these lines in 1860 and died four years later. Giallo survived for a further eight years. Hopefully, they met again in heaven.

'Foxl'

from *Hitler's Table Talk,*
1941–4

It was in January 1915 that I got hold of Foxl. He was engaged in pursuing a rat that had jumped into our trench. He fought against me, and tried to bite me, but I didn't let go. I led him back with me to the rear. He constantly tried to escape. With exemplary patience (he didn't understand a word of German), I gradually got him used to me. At first I gave him only biscuits and chocolate (he'd acquired his habits with the English, who were better fed than we were). Then I began to train him. He never went an inch from my side. At that time, my comrades had no use at all for him. Not only was I fond of the beast, but it interested me to study his reactions. I finally taught him everything: how to jump over obstacles, how to climb up a ladder and down again. The essential thing is that a dog should always sleep beside its master. When I had to go up into the line, and there was a lot of shelling, I used to tie him up in the trench. My comrades told me that he took no interest in anyone during my absence. He would recognise me even from a distance. What an outburst of enthusiasm he would let loose in my honour! We called him Foxl. He went all through the Somme, the battle of Arras. He was not at all impressionable. When I was wounded, it was Karl Lanzhammer who took care of him. On my return, he hurled himself on me in a frenzy.

When a dog looks in front of him in a vague fashion and with clouded eyes, one knows that images of the past are chasing each other through his memory.

How many times at Fromelles, during the First World War, I've studied my dog Foxl. When he came back from a walk with the huge bitch who was his companion, we found him covered with bites. We'd no sooner bandaged him, and had ceased to bother about him, than he would shake off this unwanted load. A fly began buzzing. Foxl was stretched out at my side, with his muzzle between his paws. The fly came close to him. He quivered with his eyes, as if hypnotised. His face wrinkled up and acquired an old man's expression. Suddenly he leapt forward, barked and became agitated. I used to watch him as if he'd been a man . . . the progressive stages of his anger, of the bile that took possession of him. He was a fine creature.

When I ate, he used to sit beside me and follow my gestures with

40

his gaze. If by the fifth or sixth mouthful I hadn't given him anything, he used to sit up on his rump and look at me with an air of saying: 'And what about me, am I not here at all?' It was crazy how fond I was of the beast. Nobody could touch me without Foxl's instantly becoming furious. He would follow nobody but me. When gas warfare started, I couldn't go on taking him into the front line. It was my comrades who fed him. When I returned after two days' absence, he would refuse to leave me again. Everybody in the trenches loved him. During marches he would run all round us, observing everything, not missing a detail. I used to share everything with him. In the evening he used to lie beside me.

To think that they stole him from me! I'd made a plan, if I got out of the war alive, to procure a female companion for him. I couldn't have parted from him. I've never in my life sold a dog. Foxl was a real circus dog. He knew all the tricks.

I remember, it was before we arrived at Colmar. The railway employee who coveted Foxl came again to our carriage and offered me two hundred marks. 'You could give me two hundred thousand, and you wouldn't get him!' When I left the train at Harpsheim, I suddenly noticed that the dog had disappeared. The column marched off, and it was impossible for me to stay behind! I was desperate. The swine who stole my dog doesn't realise what he did to me.

'The swine who stole my dog doesn't realise what he did to me' — and to *us!* For the writer is Hitler and he seems to have become distraught over his loss.

It may offend readers to find Hitler included here; I hope not, for that is not the intention. Surely his affection for dogs is a fascinating aspect of the man? That he was a dog lover is confirmed by the following comments:

I love animals, and especially dogs. But I'm not so very fond of boxers, for example. If I had to take a new dog, it could only be a sheepdog, preferably a bitch. I would feel like a traitor if I became attached to a dog of any other breed. What extraordinary animals they are: lively, loyal, bold, courageous and handsome! The blind man's dog is one of the most touching things in existence. He's more attached to his master than to any other dog. If he allows a bitch to distract his attention for a moment, it's for hardly any time and he has a bad conscience. With bitches it's more difficult. When they're on heat, they can't be restrained.

The dog is the oldest of domestic animals. He has been man's companion for more than thirty thousand years. But man, in his pride, is not capable of perceiving that even between dogs of the same breed there are extraordinary differences. There are stupid dogs and others who are so intelligent that it's agonising.

In many ways my sheepdog Blondi is a vegetarian. There are lots of herbs which she eats with obvious pleasure, and it is interesting to see how she turns to them if her stomach is out of order. It is astonishing to see how wise animals are, and how well they know what is good for them.

Having no hearts

SIR HUGH WALPOLE
(1884–1941)

Mr and Mrs William Thrush owned a very sweet little house in Benedict Canyon, Los Angeles. That is, the postal address was Los Angeles, but Benedict Canyon is a Hollywood district if ever there was one. The Thrushes liked it for that reason, among others, and it gave William Thrush a very real pleasure when he heard the big motor wagons, between seven and eight in the morning, thundering down the Canyon on their way to location. This was about as near as he ever got to Pictures. He didn't wish to get any nearer, because he had a certain pride; not very much, but enough to make him desire to live in a society where he would be valued. Every morning he read the columns of film-making gossip in his daily paper, and always remarked to Isabelle: 'Goodness! If they don't have a time!' Then they both felt happy and a little superior too.

Isabelle Thrush had more pride than William. In fact, she had a great deal, and she spent most of her time in feeding it or inducing other people to do so. Would you say they were a happy pair? If you didn't know all about them, certainly yes. If you did know all about them, you would probably be doubtful, as William often was. There was something wrong between Isabelle and himself, although they'd been married for ten years and very seldom squabbled about anything. They didn't quarrel, because William refused to. Isabelle had undoubtedly a shrill temper, especially when she didn't get what she wanted. Of course, she couldn't get all the things that she wanted because William, who was a clerk in one of the leading banks in Los Angeles, had but a moderate salary. It happened, however, that a wealthy aunt of his had died some three or four years before and left him a pretty little sum. He invested this wisely, so that even through the depression it remained. But Isabelle had all of it and then a little more.

He asked himself sometimes, in the privacy of the night, whether she were greedy. He couldn't be sure, because he often read in American magazines about the tyranny of the American wife and how she eagerly bled her husband. Well, Isabelle wasn't as bad as that. Gosh! He'd see to it if she tried anything like that on him. And so, he decided comfortably, she was better than most American wives. Isabelle considered herself a really magnificent creature, filled with all the virtues — courage, wisdom, self-sacrifice, love and endurance. She thought that William was extremely lucky to be married to her. And this thought produced in her a kindly, motherly air when he was around, as though she were saying: 'Little man, I'll look after you. Don't be afraid.' And then: 'How lucky really you are!'

The Thrushes had no children. That was Isabelle's wish, because she said it was wicked to bring a child into the world when you weren't going to give it everything of the best. William, once when he was feeling peevish because of his indigestion, remarked to her that his aunt's money would look after the child all right. But Isabelle was indignant, indeed, and said that there was a cruel strain in his nature which he would have to watch or he'd be a real sadist.

Having no children, Isabelle thought that it would be pleasant to have a dog. Many of her lady friends had them. There were, in fact, far more hospitals for dogs in Beverly and Hollywood than for human beings. And everybody said that the dog hospitals were so perfectly run that it was worth having a dog just for that reason alone. Isabelle wanted a dog, but there were problems to be settled. She understood that unless you had it as a puppy, it never became really fond of you. On the other hand, puppies had to be trained, and one's beautiful rugs and carpets suffered in the process. Then, what kind of dog should she have? There were the darling Cockers, the adorable Scotch Terriers, the amusing Dachshunds and the great big splendid Setters and Airedales. Some very lonely women had Pekingese, and then there were French Bulldogs. She couldn't make up her mind, and used to ask William which sort he preferred. And William, while he was trying to guess what she wanted him to say, would look at her with that slow, puzzling stare, which Isabelle always interpreted as a tribute of gratified recognition of her brilliance and beauty. In reality, what he was saying was: 'What is the matter with Isabelle? She has gone somewhere and I don't know quite where.'

They lived the social life of ladies and gentlemen of moderate means in Hollywood. That is, they went to previews of celebrated pictures; in the summer they sat in the Bowl and wiped the damp off their fingers as they listened confusedly to symphonies by Brahms and Beethoven; they occasionally, with great daring, went with a friend or two to a burlesque in Los Angeles; they played bridge quite badly and gave little dinner-parties at which the coloured maid was never quite satisfactory. On the whole, it was a happy life.

Then one day, William, sitting alone and doing a crossword puzzle in the patio of his little Spanish house, had a visitor. Isabelle was out playing bridge with some friends and he was enjoying the lovely tranquil sunset, which lay like a golden sheet let down from heaven protectingly over the Canyon. In another half-hour the light would be gone, the air would be chill and sharp and he would go indoors and read his evening newspaper, turn on the heat, and wonder why he wasn't as happy as he ought to be. Then he saw enter his little garden, through a hole in the hedge, a French bulldog.

This dog sniffed around, looked at him from a distance with a very nervous expression and then slowly advanced towards him, twisting and bending his thick body as though it were made of some elastic substance. William Thrush looked at the dog and disliked him exceedingly. He'd never had a great passion for dogs, ever since, years and years ago, his mother in a real temper had shaken him and told him he was as silly as a terrier puppy. So he'd grown up disliking dogs. And being himself a short little man, with large glasses and rather bowed legs, short dogs were especially unpleasant to him.

In any case, this dog seemed to him the ugliest ever. The dog seemed to him to be so very ugly that he felt a sort of nausea. He said, 'Shoo! Go away!' But the dog was evidently accustomed to being disliked. On looking back over this first meeting, William reflected on the fact that the dog resembled himself, in that if anyone disliked him some kind of paralysis seized him and he simply stayed and stayed, although he knew that he ought to go away. So did the dog now. He didn't come up to William, but lay at full length on the grass at a short distance and looked at him with his bulging, ugly, and in some unpleasant way, very human eyes.

William went up to him that he might frighten him out of the garden. But instead of that, the dog lay over on his back, wriggling his stomach and waving his legs feebly in the air. 'You're horrible!' William said aloud. 'I don't like dogs and never have. For God's sake, get out of here!' and then had a dreadful sense of speaking to himself — telling himself to get out of the house and garden and go somewhere. The dog turned over, sat up, gave him a beseeching but intimate look, as though he said: 'I know you much better than you think I do. Nothing could destroy our intimacy,' and then went quietly out of the garden.

His wife returned later, vexed because she had lost at bridge. 'Such cards, my dear, you would have thought there was a spell on me. I don't know what to do about it. The cards I've been having lately!' He told her about the dog, but she wasn't in the very least interested, and after her absent-minded 'Really? How revolting!' went on with a long story about a shop in Los Angeles, where you could get a mink coat, or if it wasn't mink it looked very like it, by paying so small a sum weekly that you really didn't know you were paying it.

'No, you wouldn't,' said William, who was most unexpectedly cross, 'because I should be paying it.'

This upset her very much indeed. She detested mean people, and suddenly, standing there in the garden, which the sun had left so that it was cold and dead, she realized that William *was* mean, and that she had been living with a mean man for years and years, and it was quite wonderful for her to endure it. William on his part felt, oddly enough, that she had behaved to him just as he had behaved to the dog. 'Damn that dog!' he thought to himself. 'I can't get it out of my mind.'

Next morning, however, Isabelle was in excellent temper again, and for this reason: Helena Peters rang her up on the telephone and informed her that she had the most enchanting Cocker puppy. In fact she had two, a male and a female. Which of them would Isabelle prefer? It seems that the breed was perfect and its price in any kind of market would be fifty dollars apiece, but Helena was giving this dog to Isabelle and it was an act of friendship, because she loved Isabelle so dearly.

'I don't know why she's doing it,' Isabelle said to William. 'She wants something or other. Helena never gives anything for nothing — but it sounds a perfect puppy. I'll go around for it myself this morning.'

William very feebly suggested the disadvantages of having puppies — the wear and tear, the unpleasant hidden smells, the certainty that the dog would have distemper and die and so on. Isabelle waved all these objections aside. She had cherished them herself until William mentioned them. But, as was so often the case, her brain, so superior to William's, insisted that anything that he said must be foolish. So she went around and fetched the puppy.

Standing in the doorway at lunch-time, her face rosy with

46

pleasure, the puppy lying in her arms against her dark green dress, its large amber eyes turned up to hers, its tongue suddenly licking her cheek, its soft brown body, its long silken ears, there was a picture so lovely that William, with a pang at his heart, wondered why it was that he didn't love her more dearly.

The puppy slowly turned its head towards William and looked at him. Was there in its eyes, even from the very first moment, a certain contempt? Had it hoped, young as it was, to find William someone quite different? Did its gaze wander to the incipient paunch, the bowed legs, and rise again to the round, rather pathetic face in which the eyes, William's best feature, were hidden behind the dull, gleaming glasses?

As they stood together in the cosy living-room, while the puppy wandered cautiously from table to chair, from chair to sofa, he was sure that Isabelle was above the puppy's social line, and that he, alas! was below it. The puppy sat down. 'Look out!' William cried. 'He had better be put in the garden.' Isabelle regarded him scornfully.

'*This* puppy is intelligent. Helena tells the most amazing stories about it. It isn't, technically, house-trained, of course, but it is wonderfully mature for a puppy. Helena says it avoids all the really valuable rugs.'

And the puppy did seem to be wonderfully sophisticated. Not that it wasn't a real puppy. It rushed about madly, it bit everything and everybody within sight, played with a string as though it had discovered the secret of perpetual motion at last, it went suddenly to sleep in your arms in the most adorable manner. It had everything that a puppy ought to have. The trouble was that it knew all about its charm. It was perfectly aware that when it lay on its side and grinned at you over its silken ear, it was entirely bewitching. And when it pretended to be angry, growling, showing its white little teeth and flashing its amber eyes, no-one in the world could resist it.

Isabelle insisted that it should be called Roosevelt.

'Why?' asked William.

'Well, I think he's the most wonderful man in the world, and now, when people are turning against him and saying horrid things about the New Deal and that he's a Socialist and everything of that sort, one has to stand up for him and come right out into the open.'

'I don't see', said William, 'that calling the puppy Roosevelt is coming out into the open.'

'It's a kind of demonstration. After all, isn't the puppy the sweetest thing in the world?'

'I don't think,' said William, sulkily, 'that Roosevelt would like anyone to call him the sweetest thing in the world. He isn't at all that kind of man.'

She looked at him reflectively. What had happened to him? Was it, perhaps, that she was only now really beginning to discover him? And if she discovered him a little further, how would it be then? Would she be able to endure it?

There is no doubt that after the arrival of the puppy, they bickered a good deal. A happy marriage between two persons depends altogether on mutual charity, unless one of the two is so absolutely a sheep that he doesn't mind what is done to him. Isabelle was a woman who had charity for everyone and everybody, but it was charity of a kind. It never worked unless Isabelle's pride was properly fed first. William, unfortunately, continued increasingly to look at her with that puzzled bewildered expression that is so justly irritating to wives.

And then the puppy confirmed her in her growing sense of injustice. People love dogs because they are so flattering. If you are unjust to your friend and feel a certain shame, your dog swiftly restores your self-confidence. It never knows that you have been mean or jealous or grasping. It encourages you to be kindly to itself, and when you respond, it loves you.

The puppy, Roosevelt, must have been born a courtier; its tact was perfectly astonishing. For instance, when it arrived in the bedroom in the morning and greeted the twin beds with little yelps of ecstatic pleasure, it almost at once discriminated between Isabelle's bed and William's. It went to William first so that Isabelle, looking enchanting in her early-morning sleep bewilderment, was given the opportunity to say: 'Isn't he coming to Mummy then?' and Isabelle's little smile of gratified pleasure when it rushed over to her, as though William never existed, was something delightful to witness.

When guests were present, as they often were, how Roosevelt was adored! And how then he made it appear that it was really because of Isabelle that he seemed so charming. He bit delicately at a lady's dress, or chewed playfully at the corner of a handsome purse with a side glance at Isabelle, as though he was saying to the ladies: 'It is because I love her so. It is because she is such a perfect darling. It is because I'm so wonderfully happy with her that I'm behaving like this.' William had never greatly cared for Isabelle's lady friends and generally avoided occasions when they would be present. That was one of Isabelle's complaints. But now he simply could not bear to be there. Isabelle's patronage of him was one thing, but Isabelle and Roosevelt together were more than any man could endure. And so they had a quarrel.

'You're behaving ridiculously about that dog.'

'Ridiculously?' That was something that Isabelle never would forgive. 'You've hated it,' she asserted, her eyes flashing, 'ever since its arrival. And why? Why? Shall I tell you?'

'Please do,' said William, stony-faced.

'Because it prefers me to you, because it always has.'

'Oh, damn the dog!' said William.

Meanwhile, the French bulldog made frequent appearances, but never when Isabelle was about. Greatly though William disliked it, he began, very reluctantly, to be interested in its personality. It wanted so terribly to be loved, and it was a certainty nobody loved it. Building was in process near by. And William, after he shaved in the morning, looking out of the window, would watch its approach to the different workmen, wiggling its body and leaping heavily up and down, and all the workmen repulsed it. They were good, kindly men, no doubt, as most American workmen are, but they felt about it as William did, that it was too ugly to be borne. He christened it Ugly, and as soon as he had given it a name it seemed to have at once a closer relationship with him.

'Get away, Ugly, you beastly dog!' he would say. And the dog would be apparently in an ecstasy of enjoyment at being called anything at all. Once in a fit of abstraction, sitting there wondering why it was that he was so lonely, wondering why everything was going wrong with Isabelle and what it was that she really lacked, Ugly came close to him, and not knowing what he did, he stroked its back and tickled it behind the ear. He was aware then of a wave of affection that was almost terrifying.

As soon as William realized what he had done, he moved away with an irritated murmur. The dog did not follow him, but stayed there stretched out looking at him. How unpleasant is naked sentimentality in this modern realistic world! How we run from sentiment and how right it is that we should do so! And yet William was sentimental too. Someone loved him, and although he detested the dog, he was not quite as lonely as he'd been before.

It happened, of course, that Roosevelt and Ugly had various encounters. Ugly would come across the path into the garden, and finding Roosevelt there, hoped that they might have a game. But Roosevelt, young as he was, played only with his social equals. He did not snarl at Ugly. He did nothing mean or common. He allowed Ugly supplicatingly to sniff him, to walk around him, even to cavort and prance a little, and then very quietly he strolled indoors. And then Isabelle realized that Ugly existed.

'William, do look at that hideous dog! What's it doing here? Shoo! Shoo! Get away, you horrible animal!' and Ugly went. William found himself, to his own surprise, defending Ugly.

'He isn't so bad,' he said. 'Not much to look at, of course, but friendly, obedient, rather a decent dog.'

'Oh, you would!' said Isabelle. 'It only needs the most hideous animal I've seen in my life to come your way for you to praise it. Really, William, I don't know what's happening to you.'

William smiled at her and said very gently: 'I don't know what's happening, either.' He made then, almost as though it were under Ugly's instructions, a serious attempt to persuade Isabelle to love him again. He was very patient, thoughtful, generous. A few people in the world knew that William Thrush had an extraordinary amount of charm — even a kind of penetrating wit when he liked. But William's charm was unconscious. It failed him when he tried to summon it. And now the more he tried, the more irritating to her he became.

The breach grew wider, and Isabelle confessed to her closer friends that she didn't know whether she could stand it much longer. Then, as nothing ever stays where it is but always advances to its appointed climax, the catastrophe occurred.

One of the troubles between William and Isabelle had always been that William liked to read and Isabelle did not. William liked long, long novels, preferably about family life. Novels that went on and on for ever and ever, in which you could be completely lost. Novels that deceived you with so friendly and profuse a carelessness that it was like a personal compliment to yourself. Isabelle, on the other hand, could not bear to read. She looked at the social column of the daily paper and sometimes a film magazine or a fashion monthly. But for the most part, as she said, she adored to read, but 'just didn't have the time to open a book'.

This had once been very sad to William, who in his young glowing days had imagined sitting on one side of the fire reading aloud to his dear little wife, who was sewing things for the baby, but nevertheless able to take it all in and speculate about the characters. Well, on this particular day, he was deep in a novel by one of those English novelists who have so many characters in their family that they have to have a genealogical table at the end of the book. To this same table he would often refer with a pleasing sense that he was staying in the most delightful house with an enormous family of cousins. He read cosily and comfortably. The door leading on to the porch was open and the afternoon sun poured bountifully in. He was aware then that something had occurred. There had been no sound, no movement, but looking up, he beheld a very horrible sight.

Ugly was advancing towards him, and one of his eyes, a blood-red ball, was nearly torn from his head. The dog made no sound whatever. He simply came towards William, only once and again lifting a paw feebly, as though he were absurdly puzzled as to what had happened to him. When he got near to William, he crouched down, and, still without a sound, looked up into his face.

William's first feeling was of nausea. He hated the sight of blood. His sensitive soul was intensely distressed by any kind of physical suffering. This seemed to him quite horrible. Then almost at once he was overwhelmed with pity. He'd never in his life before been so sorry for anything. Something in the distressed trusting patience of the dog won his heart completely and for ever. That the animal should be so silent, making no complaint, seemed to him himself as he ought to be. That was how he'd wish to behave had such a terrible thing happened to him. How, he was sure, he would *not* behave.

He said nothing, but arose from his chair, was about to take the dog in his arms and hasten at once with it to the nearest dog hospital, when Isabelle entered and Roosevelt scampered out from a room near by. She was smiling and happy. She greeted the cocker puppy with little cries of baby joy. 'Oh, the darling! The ickle, ickle darling! Wasn't he an angel to come and see his mummy?' And then she saw the other dog. Ugly had turned his head and was looking at her. She screamed. She put her hands in front of her face.

'Oh, William, how horrible! How frightful! It must be killed at once!'

William got up, took the heavy, bleeding dog in his arms, and without a word, passed her and went out.

51

He went into the garage, laid the dog on the old rug, got out his car, picked up the dog again, got into the car with him and drove off to the dog hospital. Here he talked to a very kindly plump little man and discussed whether Ugly should be destroyed or not. When the little man took Ugly in his arms to examine him, the dog very slowly turned his head, and, with his one eye, looked at William as much as to say: 'If you think this is the right thing for me to do, I'll suffer it.' William even nodded his head to the dog and a silent understanding seemed to pass between them.

'It seems to have no damage anywhere else,' the doctor said. 'It was done, of course, by another dog. They do that. They just take hold of one place and don't let go again. Poor old fellow!' The dog doctor caressed him. 'Not very handsome, anyway, is he?'

'Oh, I don't know,' said William; 'he's got a kind of character about him, I think.'

'Is he your dog?' asked the doctor.

'No. I don't think he belongs to anybody, but he comes to our garden sometimes. I've grown interested in him.'

'Well, I can tell you this,' the doctor said, 'I guess he'll be all right. We can sew it up so you'll hardly notice it. He won't exactly be a beauty, you know.'

'Yes, I know,' said William, who wasn't a beauty either. He went home.

For some reason or another, Isabelle had been greatly excited by the incident. She sat there and gave William a terrific lecture, the total of which was that for ever so long now he'd been letting himself go. He was becoming soppy, almost a sissy, in fact.

'A sissy?' said William, indignantly.

'Oh, well, you know what I mean. You're getting dreadfully sentimental. You always had a tendency that way, but lately it's been terrible. All my friends notice it.'

I don't know why it is, but there is almost nothing so irritating in the world as to be told by someone that one's friends have been silently, mysteriously, observing one to one's disadvantage. William, for the first time in their married life, lost all control of himself. He stood up and raved. He said that it didn't matter whether he was getting sentimental or not, but anyway, perhaps sentiment wasn't a bad thing. What really mattered was that Isabelle was selfish, cold and unkind! That she hadn't any idea of the horrible woman she was becoming. Isabelle suitably replied. In fact, they both thoroughly lost their tempers. And while this was going on, Roosevelt sat in Isabelle's lap making little playful bites at Isabelle's dress and beautiful fingers. While he sat there, he looked at William with a really terrible sarcasm in his soft, amber eyes — sarcasm and scorn.

'I tell you what,' William cried in a last frenzy, 'I hate that dog! Puppies ought to be nice, gentle, loving creatures. Look at him! He's hard as iron and the most horrid snob.'

So then Isabelle burst into tears, went to her room and locked her door. There followed days of constrained silence, and after that William went down to the dog hospital.

'He's a patient dog, I must say,' the doctor remarked. 'Never a whine. Seems fond of you too.'

William was surprised at the pleasure that he felt at the tribute. The day came when Ugly's eye was gone, the empty space sewed up, and his whole air rather that of a drunken soldier who had been in the wars. What was to be done with him? William, realizing that the crisis of his life was upon him, decided that if Isabelle had her Roosevelt, he should have his Ugly. He went home and told her so. This was at breakfast. She said no word and he left for his work in the city.

When he returned in the late afternoon there was a strange silence about the house. He had been thinking and had decided that in some way or another this awful trouble with Isabelle must be stopped. After all, surely he loved her. Or if he didn't, they were at least man and wife. How miserable, how lost, he would be without her! Would he? At that appalling wonder, his whole soul shook. So he returned home with every intention of making everything all right again, although how he was to do that he didn't in the least know.

Ugly greeted him, coming in from the garden, rolling his body about, baring his teeth, showing an ecstasy of pleasure, But Isabelle was not there, nor Roosevelt. On his writing-table lay the note so essential to all dramatists and novelists who have learnt their job. What it said was that Isabelle had gone to her mother in Santa Barbara and would remain there. She wished that William would give her a divorce. She had been seeing for a long time how impossible things were. She had taken Roosevelt with her.

William read the note and felt a dreadful shame and despair. His impulse was to depart at once for Santa Barbara. And so he would have done if it had not been for Ugly. But he could not leave him just then. The dog was new to the house and the servants had no especial affection for him. In a day or two he would go. But he did not. The days passed and he did not.

A quite terrible thing happened to him. He found that he liked the house better without Isabelle than with her. He found that he adored his freedom. That he could now have liberty of action and thought, that showed him what all these years he'd been missing. He discovered a number of other things. He took long walks up the Canyon with Ugly. He talked to the dog and it seemed to him that the dog answered him. Strangest of all, he was less lonely than he had been when Isabelle was there. It was as though for years there had been a padlock on his mind. Someone, something, had all the time inhibited his thought.

A letter came from Isabelle and he made his discovery. In her letter she said she was now ready to return. Santa Barbara wasn't half the place it had once been, and her mother was in many ways unsympathetic, and, he would be glad to hear, she missed her dear old William. As he wrote his reply to her letter, he solved his problem. This was the letter he wrote.

Dear Isabelle,

'I don't want you to come back. This sounds very unkind and rude on my part, but I've done a lot of thinking in the last few weeks and I know that I must be honest. For a long while I've been wondering what it was that was wrong between us. I admire you so much. You are far finer than I. You have been so good and so kind for so long, that it seems absurd to say that you are lacking in anything. But you are. You have no heart. That sounds like a thing you read in a novel, but I mean it just like that. I don't think you're any the worse for not having one — it is only that I have suddenly discovered while I've been alone here that that is the one real difference between human beings. Either you have a heart, or you haven't one. What I mean is, either the heart is the part of your body that functions more than any other or not. This is the one insuperable difference between people. Not whether you're a Fascist or Communist, American or French, teetotaller or a drunkard, clever or stupid. All those things can be got over quite easily. I'm not saying either that the people with hearts are preferable to those without. I think it is possibly just the opposite. The people with hearts are nearly always too sentimental, too emotional, prevent the work of the world being done, get in the way of the real thinkers. The people without hearts are, as the world is now going, the ones we really want. But the difference is there. I can't help feeling emotionally about things. You can't help the opposite. But we mustn't live together any more. This is a difference that nothing can get over.'

'Yours sincerely,

'William'

'PS. — There is the same difference between Roosevelt and Ugly.'

When he had posted the letter and was walking in a last cool flash of sunshine up the Canyon, Ugly ambling along beside him, he thought that possibly no-one had ever written so silly a letter. And yet, he had this sense that he had made this marvellous discovery. He looked at all his friends, male and female, and saw the dividing line with absolute clearness. He looked beyond the other great figures in the world. Einstein had a heart — Hitler, even. On the other hand, Mussolini possibly not. And Simon Callahan, the manager of his bank in Los Angeles, most certainly not! Ugly, whose vision of course was now sadly dimmed, saw a golden leaf, one of the first signs of autumn, twirling through the air. He leapt rather foolishly, ran a little way and looked back at William. William smiled encouragement. Then he turned back home, Ugly delightedly following.

Call of the wild

That wild dogs kill is a brute fact of nature. And they do so nastily. *The Spectator* described the wild dogs of India, (in 1893):

> Having found their tiger they proceed, not to attack him at once, but to starve him until they have materially reduced his strength. Night and day they form a cordon round the unfortunate beast, and allow him no chance of obtaining food or rest; every time the tiger essays to break the circle, this is widened as the pack flies before him, only to relentlessly narrow again when the quarry is exhausted. After a certain period of this treatment the tiger falls a comparatively easy prey to his active and persevering enemies. This theory of their plan of attack, while it may detract somewhat from the wild dog's reputation for courage, must add considerably to our estimate of their intelligence.

The sagacity of dogs, at their most cunning.

Here are three stories: the first, from *Death in the Woods and Other Stories,* by the American novelist Sherwood Anderson, describes dogs gone wild; the other two are extracts from one of the finest dog books ever written, *Jock of the Bushveld,* by Sir Percy Fitzpatrick, which shows the dog as hunter on behalf of his master. The stories take place in Africa.

Death in the woods
SHERWOOD ANDERSON
(1876–1941)

They left everything at home for her to manage and she had no money. She knew no one. No one ever talked to her in town. When it was Winter she had to gather sticks of wood for her fire, had to try to keep the stock fed with very little grain.

The stock in the barn cried to her hungrily, the dogs followed her about. In the Winter the hens laid few enough eggs. They huddled in the corners of the barn and she kept watching them. If a hen lays an egg in the barn in the Winter and you do not find it, it freezes and breaks.

One day in Winter the old woman went off to town with a few eggs and the dogs followed her. She did not get started until nearly three o'clock and the snow was heavy. She hadn't been feeling very well for several days and so she went muttering along, scantily clad, her shoulders stooped. She had an old grain bag in which she carried her eggs, tucked away down in the bottom. There weren't many of them, but in Winter the price of eggs is up. She would get a little meat in exchange for the eggs, some salt pork, a little sugar, and some coffee perhaps. It might be the butcher would give her a piece of liver.

When she had got to town and was trading in her eggs the dogs lay by the door outside. She did pretty well, got the things she needed, more than she had hoped. Then she went to the butcher and he gave her some liver and some dog-meat.

It was the first time any one had spoken to her in a friendly way for a long time. The butcher was alone in his shop when she came in and was annoyed by the thought of such a sick-looking old woman out on such a day. It was bitter cold and the snow, that had let up during the afternoon, was falling again. The butcher said something about her husband and her son, swore at them, and the old woman stared at him, a look of mild surprise in her eyes as he talked. He said that if either the husband or the son were going to get any of the liver or the heavy bones with scraps of meat hanging to them that he had put into the grain bag, he'd see him starve first.

Starve, eh? Well, things had to be fed. Men had to be fed, and the horses that weren't any good but maybe could be traded off, and the poor thin cow that hadn't given any milk for three months.

Horses, cows, pigs, dogs, men.

The old woman had to get back before darkness came if she could. The dogs followed at her heels, sniffing at the heavy grain bag she had fastened on her back. When she got to the edge of town she stopped by a fence and tied the bag on her back with a piece of rope she had carried in her dress-pocket for just that purpose. That was an easier way to carry it. Her arms ached. It was hard when she had to crawl over fences and once she fell over and landed in the snow. The dogs went frisking about. She had to struggle to get to her feet again, but she made it. The point of climbing over the fences was that there was a short cut over a hill and through a wood. She might have gone around by the road, but it was a mile farther that way. She was afraid she couldn't make it. And then, besides, the stock had to be fed. There was a little hay left and a little corn. Perhaps her husband and son would bring some home when they came. They had driven off in the only buggy the Grimes family had, a rickety thing, a rickety horse hitched to the buggy, two other rickety horses led by halters. They were going to trade horses, get a little money if they could. They might come home drunk. It would be well to have something in the house when they came back.

The son had an affair on with a woman at the county seat, fifteen miles away. She was a rough enough woman, a tough one. Once, in the Summer, the son had brought her to the house. Both she and the son had been drinking. Jake Grimes was away and the son and his woman ordered the old woman about like a servant. She didn't mind much; she was used to it. Whatever happened she never said anything. That was her way of getting along. She had managed that way when she was a young girl at the German's and ever since she had married Jake. That time her son brought his woman to the house they stayed all night, sleeping together just as though they were married. It hadn't shocked the old woman, not much. She had got past being shocked early in life.

With the pack on her back she went painfully along across an open field, wading in the deep snow, and got into the woods.

There was a path, but it was hard to follow. Just beyond the top of the hill, where the woods was thickest, there was a small clearing. Had someone once thought of building a house there? The clearing was as large as a building lot in town, large enough for a house and a garden. The path ran along the side of the clearing, and when she got there the old woman sat down to rest at the foot of a tree.

It was a foolish thing to do. When she got herself placed, the pack against the tree's trunk, it was nice, but what about getting up again? She worried about that for a moment and then quietly closed her eyes.

She must have slept for a time. When you are about so cold you can't get any colder. The afternoon grew a little warmer and the snow came thicker than ever. Then after a time the weather cleared. The moon even came out.

There were four Grimes dogs that had followed Mrs. Grimes into town, all tall gaunt fellows. Such men as Jake Grimes and his son always keep just such dogs. They kick and abuse them, but they stay. The Grimes dogs, in order to keep from starving, had to do a lot of foraging for themselves, and they had been at it while the old woman slept with her back to the tree at the side of the clearing. They had been chasing rabbits in the woods and in adjoining fields and in their ranging had picked up three other farm dogs.

After a time all the dogs came back to the clearing. They were excited about something. Such nights, cold and clear and with a moon, do things to dogs. It may be that some old instinct, come down from the time when they were wolves and ranged the woods in packs on Winter nights, comes back into them.

The dogs in the clearing, before the old woman, had caught two or three rabbits and their immediate hunger had been satisfied. They began to play, running in circles in the clearing. Round and round they ran, each dog's nose at the tail of the next dog. In the clearing, under the snow-laden trees and under the wintry moon they made a strange picture, running thus silently, in a circle their running had beaten in the soft snow. The dogs made no sound. They ran around and around in the circle.

It may have been that the old woman saw them doing that before she died. She may have awakened once or twice and looked at the strange sight with dim old eyes.

She wouldn't be very cold now, just drowsy. Life hangs on a long time. Perhaps the old woman was out of her head. She may have dreamed of her girlhood, at the German's, and before that, when she was a child and before her mother lit out and left her.

Her dreams couldn't have been very pleasant. Not many pleasant things had happened to her. Now and then one of the Grimes dogs left the running circle and came to stand before her. The dog thrust his face close to her face. His red tongue was hanging out.

The running of the dogs may have been a kind of death ceremony. It may have been that the primitive instinct of the wolf, having been aroused in the dogs by the night and the running, made them somehow afraid.

'Now we are no longer wolves. We are dogs, the servants of men. Keep alive, man! When man dies we become wolves again.'

When one of the dogs came to where the old woman sat with her back against the tree and thrust his nose close to her face he seemed satisfied and went back to run with the pack. All the Grimes dogs did it at some time during the evening, before she died. I knew all about it afterward, when I grew to be a man, because once in a woods in Illinois, on another Winter night, I saw a pack of dogs act just like that. The dogs were waiting for me to die as they had waited for the old woman that night when I was a child, but when it happened to me I was a young man and had no intention whatever of dying.

The old woman died softly and quietly. When she was dead and when one of the Grimes dogs had come to her and had found her dead all the dogs stopped running.

They gathered about her.

Well, she was dead now. She had fed the Grimes dogs when she was alive, what about now?

There was the pack on her back, the grain bag containing the piece of salt pork, the liver the butcher had given her, the dog-meat, the soup bones. The butcher in town, having been suddenly overcome with a feeling of pity, had loaded her grain bag heavily. It had been a big haul for the old woman.

It was a big haul for the dogs now.

One of the Grimes dogs sprang suddenly out from among the others and began worrying the pack on the old woman's back. Had the dogs really been wolves that one would have been the leader of the pack. What he did, all the others did.

All of them sank their teeth into the grain bag the old woman has fastened with ropes to her back.

They dragged the old woman's body out into the open clearing. The worn-out dress was quickly torn from her shoulders. When she was found, a day or two later, the dress had been torn from her body clear to the hips, but the dogs had not touched her body. They had got the meat out of the grain bag, that was all. Her body was frozen stiff when it was found, and the shoulders were so narrow and the body so slight that in death it looked like the body of some charming young girl.

Such things happened in towns of the Middle West, on farms near town, when I was a boy.

Jess
SIR PERCY FITZPATRICK

Good dogs were not easy to get; I had tried hard enough for one before starting, but without success. Even unborn puppies had jealous prospective owners waiting to claim them.

There is always plenty of room at the top of the tree, and good hunting dogs were as rare as good men, good horses, and good front-oxen. A lot of qualities are needed in the make-up of a good hunting dog: size, strength, quickness, scent, sense and speed — and plenty of courage. They are very very difficult to get; but even small dogs are useful, and many a fine feat stands to the credit of little terriers in guarding camps at night and in standing off wounded animals that meant mischief.

Dennison was saved from a wounded lioness by his two fox terriers. He had gone out to shoot bush-pheasants, and came unexpectedly on a lioness playing with her cubs: the cubs hid in the grass, but she stood up at bay to protect them, and he, forgetting that he had taken the big 'looper' cartridges from his gun and reloaded with No. 6, fired. The shot only maddened her, and she charged; but the two dogs dashed at her, one at each side, barking, snapping and yelling, rushing in and jumping back so fast and furiously that they flustered her. Leaving the man for the moment, she turned on them, dabbing viciously with her huge paws, first at one, then at the other; quick as lightning she struck right and left as a kitten will at a twirled string; but they kept out of reach. It only lasted seconds, but that was long enough for the man to reload and shoot the lioness through the heart.

There was only the one dog in our camp; and she was not an attractive one. She was a bull terrier with a dull brindled coat — black and grey in shadowy stripes. She had small cross-looking eyes and uncertain always-moving ears; she was bad-tempered and most unsociable; but she was as faithful and as brave a dog as ever lived. She never barked; never howled when beaten for biting strangers or kaffirs or going for the cattle; she was very silent, very savage, and very quick. She belonged to my friend Ted, and never left his side day or night. Her name was Jess.

Jess was not a favourite, but everybody respected her, partly because you knew she would not stand any nonsense — no pushing, patting or punishment, and very little talking to — and partly because she was so faithful and plucky. She was not a hunting dog, but on several occasions had helped to pull down wounded game; she had no knowledge or skill, and was only fierce and brave, and there was always the risk that she would be killed. She would listen to Ted, but to no one else; one of us might have shouted his lungs out, but it would not have stopped her from giving chase the moment she saw anything and keeping on till she was too dead beat to move any further.

The first time I saw Jess we were having dinner, and I gave her a bone—putting it down close to her and saying, 'Here! good dog!' As she did not even look at it, I moved it right under her nose. She gave a low growl, and her little eyes turned on me for just one look as she got up and walked away.

There was a snigger of laughter from some of the others, but nobody said anything, and it seemed wiser to ask no questions just then. Afterwards, when we were alone, one of them told me Ted had trained her not to feed from any one else, adding, 'You must not feed another man's dog; a dog has only one master!'

We respected Jess greatly; but no one knew quite how much we respected her until the memorable day near Ship Mountain.

We had rested through the heat of the day under a big tree on the bank of a little stream; it was the tree under which Soltké prayed and died. About sundown, just before we were ready to start, some other waggons passed, and Ted, knowing the owner, went on with him, intending to rejoin us at the next outspan. As he jumped on to the passing waggon he called to Jess, and she ran out of a patch of soft grass under one of the big trees behind our waggons. She answered his call instantly, but when she saw him moving off on the other waggon she sat down in the road and watched him anxiously for some seconds, then ran on a few steps in her curious quick silent way and again stopped, giving swift glances alternately towards Ted and towards us. Ted remarked laughingly that she evidently thought he had made a mistake by getting on to the wrong waggon, and that she would follow presently.

After he had disappeared she ran back to her patch of grass and lay down, but in a few minutes she was back again squatting in the road looking with that same anxious worried expression after her master. Thus she went to and fro for the quarter of an hour it took us to inspan, and each time she passed we could hear a faint anxious little whine.

The oxen were inspanned and the last odd things were being put up when one of the boys came to say that he could not get the guns

62

and water-barrel because Jess would not let him near them. There was something the matter with the dog, he said; he thought she was mad.

Knowing how Jess hated kaffirs we laughed at the notion, and went for the things ourselves. As we came within five yards of the tree where we had left the guns there was a rustle in the grass, and Jess came out with her swift silent run, appearing as unexpectedly as a snake does, and with some odd suggestion of a snake in her look and attitude. Her head, body and tail were in a dead line, and she was crouching slightly as for a spring; her ears were laid flat back, her lips twitching constantly, showing the strong white teeth, and her cross wicked eyes had such a look of remorseless cruelty in them that we stopped as if we had been turned to stone. She never moved a muscle or made a sound, but kept those eyes steadily fixed on us. We moved back a pace or two and began to coax and wheedle her; but it was no good; she never moved or made a sound, and the unblinking look remained. For a minute we stood our ground, and then the hair on her back and shoulders began very slowly to stand up. That was enough: we cleared off. It was a mighty uncanny appearance.

Then another tried his hand; but it was just the same. No one could do anything with her; no one could get near the guns or the water-barrel; as soon as we returned for a fresh attempt she reappeared in the same place and in the same way.

The position was too ridiculous, and we were at our wits' end, for Jess held the camp. The kaffirs declared the dog was mad, and we began to have very uncomfortable suspicions that they were right; but we decided to make a last attempt, and surrounding the place approached from all sides. But the suddenness with which she appeared before we got into position so demoralised the kaffirs that they bolted, and we gave it up, owning ourselves beaten. We turned to watch her as she ran back for the last time, and as she disappeared in the grass we heard distinctly the cry of a very young puppy. Then the secret of Jess's madness was out.

We had to send for Ted, and when he returned a couple of hours later Jess met him out on the road in the dark where she had been watching half the time ever since he left. She jumped up at his chest giving a long tremulous whimper of welcome, and then ran ahead straight to the nest in the grass.

He took a lantern and we followed, but not too close. When he knelt down to look at the puppies she stood over them and pushed herself in between him and them; when he put out a hand to touch them she pushed it away with her nose, whining softly in protest and trembling with excitement — you could see she would not bite, but she hated him to touch her puppies. Finally, when he picked one up she gave a low cry and caught his wrist gently, but held it.

That was Jess, the mother of Jock!

The Koodoo Bull
SIR PERCY FITZPATRICK

Jock had learned one very clever trick in pulling down wounded animals. It often happens when you come unexpectedly upon game that they are off before you see them, and the only chance you have of getting anything is with a running shot. If they go straight from you the shot is not a very difficult one, although you see nothing but the lifting and falling hind-quarters as they canter away; and a common result of such a shot is the breaking of one of the hindlegs between the hip and the hock. Jock made his discovery while following a rietbuck which I had wounded in this way. He had made several tries at its nose and throat, but the buck was going too strongly and was out of reach; moreover it would not stop or turn when he headed it, but charged straight on, bounding over him. In trying once more for the throat he cannoned against the buck's shoulder and was sent rolling yards away. This seemed to madden him: racing up behind he flew at the dangling leg, caught it at the shin, and thrusting his feet well out, simply dragged until the buck slowed down, and then began furiously tugging sideways. The crossing of the legs brought the wounded animal down immediately and Jock had it by the throat before it could rise again.

Every one who is good at anything has some favourite method or device of his own: that was Jock's. It may have come to him, as it comes to many, by accident; but having once got it, he perfected it and used it whenever it was possible. Only once he made a mistake; and he paid for it — very nearly with his life.

He had already used this device successfully several times, but so far only with the smaller buck. This day he did what I should have thought to be impossible for a dog of three or four times his size. I left the scene of torn carcass and crunched bones, consumed by regrets and disappointment; each fresh detail only added to my feeling of disgust, but Jock did not seem to mind; he jumped out briskly as soon as I started walking in earnest, as though he recognised that we were making a fresh start and he began to look forward immediately.

The little bare flat where the koodoo had fallen for the last time was at the head of one of those depressions which collect the waters of the summer floods and, changing gradually into shallow valleys, are eventually scoured out and become the dongas — dry in winter but full charged with muddy flood in summer — which drain the Bushveld to its rivers. Here and there where an impermeable rock formation crosses these channels there are deep pools which, except in years of drought, last all through the winter; and these are the drinking-places of the game. I followed this one down for a couple of miles without any definite purpose until the sight of some greener and denser wild figs suggested that there might be water, and perhaps a rietbuck or a duiker nearby. As we reached the trees Jock showed unmistakable signs of interest in something, and with the utmost caution I moved from tree to tree in the shady grove towards where it seemed the water-hole might be.

There were bushy wild plums flanking the grove, and beyond them the ordinary scattered thorns. As I reached this point, and stopped to look out between the bushes on to the more open ground, a koodoo cow walked quietly up the slope from the water, but before there was time to raise the rifle her easy stride had carried her behind a small mimosa tree. I took one quick step out to follow her up and found myself face to face at less than a dozen yards with a grand koodoo bull. It is impossible to convey in words any real idea of the scene and how things happened. Of course it was only for a fraction of a second that we looked straight into each other's eyes; then, as if by magic, he was round and going from me with the overwhelming rush of speed and strength and weight combined. Yet it is the first sight that remains with me: the proud head, the huge spiral horns, and the wide soft staring eyes — before the wildness of panic had stricken them. The picture seems photographed on eye and brain, never to be forgotten. A whirlwind of dust and leaves marked his course, and through it I fired, unsteadied by excitement and hardly able to see. Then the right hind-leg swung out and the great creature sank for a moment, almost to the ground; and the sense of triumph, the longed for and unexpected success, 'went to my head' like a rush of blood.

There had been no time to aim, and the shot — a real snap shot — was not at all a bad one. It was after that that the natural effect of such a meeting and such a chance began to tell. Thinking it all out beforehand does not help much, for things never happen as they are expected to; and even months of practice among the smaller kinds will not ensure a steady nerve when you just come face to face with big game — there seems to be too much at stake.

I fired again as the koodoo recovered himself, but he was then seventy or eighty yards away and partly hidden at times by trees and scrub. He struck up the slope, following the line of the troop through the scattered thorns, and there, running hard and dropping quickly to my knee for steadier aim, I fired again and again — but each time a longer shot and more obscured by the intervening bush; and no tell-tale thud came back to cheer me on.

Forgetting the last night's experience, forgetting everything except how we had twice chased and twice lost them, seeing only another and the grandest prize slipping away, I sent Jock on and followed as fast as I could. Once more the koodoo came in sight — just a chance at four hundred yards as he reached an open space on rising ground. Jock was already closing up, but still unseen, and the noble old fellow turned full broadside to me as he stopped to look back. Once more I knelt, gripping hard and holding my breath to snatch a moment's steadiness, and fired; but I missed again, and as the bullet struck under him he plunged forward and disappeared over the rise at the moment that Jock, dashing out from the scrub, reached his heels.

The old Martini carbine had one bad fault; even I could not deny that; years of rough and careless treatment in all sorts of weather — for it was only a discarded old Mounted Police weapon — had told on it, and both in barrel and breech it was well pitted with rust scars. One result of this was that it was always jamming, and unless the cartridges were kept well greased the empty shells would stick and the ejector fail to work; and this was almost sure to happen when the carbine became hot from quick firing. It jammed now, and fearing to lose sight of the chase I dared not stop a second, but ran on, struggling from time to time to wrench the breach open.

Reaching the place where they had disappeared, I saw with intense relief and excitement Jock and the koodoo having it out less than a hundred yards away. The koodoo's leg was broken right up in the ham, and it was a terrible handicap for an animal so big and heavy, but his nimbleness and quickness were astonishing. Using the sound hind-leg as a pivot he swung round, always facing his enemy; Jock was in and out, here, there and everywhere, as a buzzing fly torments one on a hot day; and indeed, to the koodoo just then he was the fly and nothing more; he could only annoy his big enemy, and was playing with his life to do it. Sometimes he tried to get round; sometimes pretended to charge straight in, stopping himself with all four feet spread — just out of reach; then like a red streak he would fly through the air with a snap for the koodoo's nose. It was a fight for life and a grand sight; for the koodoo, in spite of his wound, easily held his own. No doubt he had fought out many a life and death struggle to win and hold his place as lord of the herd and knew every trick of attack and defence. Maybe too he was blazing with anger and contempt for this persistent little gadfly that worried him so and kept out of reach. Sometimes he snorted and feinted to charge; at other times backed slowly, giving way to draw the enemy on; then with a sudden lunge the great horns swished like a scythe with a tremendous reach out, easily covering the spot where Jock had been a fraction of a second before. There were pauses too in which he watched his tormentor steadily, with occasional impatient shakes of the head, or, raising it to full height, towered up a monument of splendid and contemptuous indifference, looking about with big angry but unfrightened eyes for the herd — his herd — that had deserted him; or with a slight toss of his head he would walk limpingly forward, forcing the ignored Jock before him; then, interrupted and annoyed by a flying snap at his nose, he would spring forward and strike with the sharp cloven fore-foot — zip-zip-zip — at Jock as he landed. Any one of the vicious flashing stabs would have pinned him to the earth and finished him; but Jock was never there.

Keeping what cover there was I came up slowly behind them, struggling and using all the force I dared, short of smashing the lever, to get the empty cartridge out. At last one of the turns in the fight brought me in view, and the koodoo dashed off again. For a little way the pace seemed as great as ever, but it soon died away; the driving power was gone; the strain and weight on the one sound leg and the tripping of the broken one were telling; and from then on I was close enough to see it all. In the first rush the koodoo seemed to dash right over Jock — the swirl of dust and leaves and the bulk of the koodoo hiding him; then I saw him close abreast looking up at it and making furious jumps for its nose, alternately from one side and the other, as they raced along together. The koodoo, holding its nose high and well forward, as they do when on the move, with the horns thrown back almost horizontally, was out of his reach and galloped heavily on completely ignoring his attacks.

There is a suggestion of grace and poise in the movement of the koodoo bull's head as he gallops through the bush which is one of his distinctions above the other antelopes. The same supple balancing movement that one notes in the native girls bearing their calabashes of water upon their heads is seen in the neck of the koodoo, and for the same reason: the movements of the body are softened into mere undulations, and the head with its immense spiral horns seems to sail along in voluntary company — indeed almost as though it were bearing the body below.

At the fourth or fifth attempt by Jock a spurt from the koodoo brought him cannoning against its shoulder, and he was sent rolling unnoticed yards away. He scrambled instantly to his feet, but found himself again behind: it may have been this fact that inspired the next attempt, or perhaps he realised that attack in front was useless; for this time he went determinedly for the broken leg. It swung about in wild eccentric curves, but at the third or fourth attempt he got it and hung on; and with all fours spread he dragged along the ground. The first startled spring of the koodoo jerked him into the air; but there was no let go now, and although dragged along the rough ground and dashed about among the scrub, sometimes swinging in the air, and sometimes sliding on his back, he pulled from side to side in futile attempts to throw the big animal. Ineffectual and even hopeless as it looked at first, Jock's attacks soon began to tell; the koodoo made wild efforts to get at him, but with every turn he turned too, and did it so vigorously that the staggering animal swayed over and had to plunge violently to recover its balance. So they turned this way and that, until a wilder plunge swung Jock off his feet, throwing the broken leg across the other one; then, with feet firmly planted, Jock tugged again, and the koodoo trying to regain its footing was tripped by the crossed legs and came down with a crash.

As it fell Jock was round and fastened on the nose; but it was no duiker, impala or rietbuck that he had to deal with this time. The koodoo gave a snort of indignation and shook its head: as a terrier shakes a rat, so it shook Jock, whipping the ground with his swinging body, and with another indignant snort and toss of the head flung him off, sending him skidding along the ground on his back. The koodoo had fallen on the wounded leg and failed to rise with the first effort; Jock while still slithering along the ground on

68

his back was tearing at the air with his feet in his mad haste to get back to the attack, and as he scrambled up, he raced in again with head down and the little eyes black with fury. He was too mad to be wary, and my heart stood still as the long horns went round with a swish; one black point seemed to pierce him through and through, showing a foot out the other side, and a jerky twist of the great head sent him twirling like a tip-cat eight or ten feet up in the air. It had just missed him, passing under his stomach next to the hind-legs; but, until he dropped with a thud and, tearing and scrambling to his feet, he raced in again, I felt certain he had been gored through.

The koodoo was up again then. I had rushed in with rifle clubbed, with the wild idea of stunning it before it could rise, but was met by the lowered horns and unmistakable signs of charging, and beat a retreat quite as speedy as my charge.

It was a running fight from then on: the instant the koodoo turned to go Jock was on to the leg again, and nothing could shake his hold. I had to keep at a respectful distance, for the bull was still good for a furious charge, even with Jock hanging on, and eyed me in the most unpromising fashion whenever I attempted to head it off or even to come close up.

The big eyes were bloodshot then, but there was no look of fear in them — they blazed with baffled rage. Impossible as it seemed to shake Jock off or to get away from us, and in spite of the broken leg and loss of blood, the furious attempts to beat us off did not slacken. It was a desperate running fight, and right bravely he fought it to the end.

Partly barring the way in front were the whitened trunks and branches of several trees struck down by some storm of the year before, and running ahead of the koodoo I made for these, hoping to find a stick straight enough for a ramrod to force the empty cartridge out. As I reached them the koodoo made for me with half a dozen plunges that sent me flying off for other cover; but the broken leg swayed over one of the branches, and Jock with feet planted against the tree hung on; and the koodoo, turning furiously on him, stumbled, floundered, tripped, and came down with a crash amongst the crackling wood. Once more like a flash Jock was over the fallen body and had fastened on the nose — but only to be shaken worse than before. The koodoo literally flogged the ground with him, and for an instant I shut my eyes; it seemed as if the plucky dog would be beaten into pulp. The bull tried to chop him with its fore-feet, but could not raise itself enough, and at each pause, Jock, with his watchful little eyes ever on the alert, dodged his body round to avoid the chopping feet without letting go his hold. Then with a snort of fury the koodoo, half-rising, gave its head a wild upward sweep, and shook. As a springing rod flings a fish, the koodoo flung Jock over its head and on to a low flat-topped thorn tree behind. The dog somersaulted slowly as he circled in the air, dropped on his back in the thorns some twelve feet from the ground, and came tumbling down through the branches. Surely the tree saved him, for it seemed as if such a throw must break his back. As it was he dropped with a sickening thump; yet even as he fell I saw again the scrambling tearing movement, as if he was trying to race back to the fight even before he reached ground. With a pause to breathe or even to look, he was in again, and trying once more for the nose.

The koodoo lying partly on its side, with both hind-legs hampered by the mass of dead wood, could not rise, but it swept the clear space in front with the terrible horns, and for some time kept Jock at bay. I tried stick after stick for a ramrod, but without success; at last, in desperation at seeing Jock once more hanging to the koodoo's nose, I hooked the lever on to a branch and setting my foot against the tree wrenched until the empty cartridge flew out, and I went staggering backwards.

In the last struggle, while I was busy with the rifle, the koodoo had moved, and it was then lying against one of the fallen trunks. The first swing to get rid of Jock had literally slogged him against the tree; the second swing swept him under it where a bend in the trunk raised it about a foot from the ground, and gaining his foothold there Jock stood fast — there, there, with his feet planted firmly and his shoulder humped against the dead tree, he stood this tug-of-war. The koodoo with its head twisted back, as caught at the end of the swing, could put no weight to the pull; yet the wrenches it gave to free itself drew the nose and upper lip out like tough rubber and seemed to stretch Jock's neck visibly. I had to come round within a few feet of them to avoid risk of hitting Jock, and it seemed impossible for bone and muscle to stand the two or three terrible wrenches that I saw. The shot was the end; and as the splendid head dropped slowly over, Jock let go his hold.

He had not uttered a sound except the grunts that were knocked out of him.

Friendship between dogs

There are many stories of friendships between dogs. One that delighted the Victorians was reported in *The Illustrated London News* in 1888. On a Sunday morning a hospital porter heard a dog barking at the door: 'He, though a kindly man, thought of his patients, and went to drive the dog away. Instead of finding one dog, he found three. Two white-and-tan fox terriers were standing up on the top flight of steps, while a long-haired collie lay beside them, looking very sorrowful for he was sorely wounded, and lay in a thick pool of blood. The moment the good porter showed his face the two terriers bolted, leaving their lame companion at the door. At this moment a medical student came in, and he at once treated the collie as an ordinary patient.'

The hospital was King's College, and the incident caused such a local sensation that an 'eminent dog painter', Mr Yates Carrington, went down to investigate. (The story would be nicer, of course, if the 'dog painter' happened to be a greyhound with the talent of a Royal Academician.) Anyhow, Mr Carrington verified the story, found the bloodstains and even the actual dogs whom he persuaded to pose for him:

You see the three dogs were evidently in the habit of meeting one another, for two lived close by the hospital, and the third often passed it. They were playing together on the Sunday morning. The collie cut his foot, and his little friends induced him to follow them to the outpatients' door of the hospital. The interesting point to me was that the dogs took their shortest cut through the various alleys past the back entrance to the hospital to the *front door,* mind you. The conclusion I

71

came to was that the terrier had constantly seen patients carried in that way. The end of it all was that I got the drover to lend me the collie, and was also able to borrow the terriers. The collie was the most intelligent dog-sitter I have ever had. "Jack", one of the terriers, did not approve of studio life, for on the fourth morning after his arrival here my servant informed me that he had vanished. Little thinking that "Jack", who lived four miles away, and had never been up in St John's Wood before, had been cute enough to find his way through Marylebone and Holborn, I wired his master, and received the reply that "Jack" arrived safely at 6.30 a.m. barking for admission in time for breakfast.

Subsequently, the *Outpatient* was exhibited at the Academy and purchased by Messrs Pears.

When there are several dogs in the house together a touch of jealousy is natural. A characteristic incident was recorded in *The Spectator* 1895 under the heading 'A dog that scorned to be jealous'. The author was the owner of a large, beautiful bulldog called Rose and a less lovely mongrel called Fan. A particular shawl was considered sacred by Fan and she would allow no one to touch it, Rose least of all. Fan was possessive and her moment of bliss was to lie, curled up in the arms of her mistress, when she had gone to bed. Anyone who approached was growled at, especially Rose. It should be added that Fan was a grandmother and the beautiful Rose a newcomer.

One day, in a chase of youthful exuberance, Rose misjudged the height of a gate and spiked herself badly when she jumped over it. Returning home after ten days in the care of the vet she was welcomed by Fan, but the family feared the worst when Rose proceeded upstairs to the bedroom and leapt into the sacred spot on the bed in a rapture of relief. Fan flew after her, but, to everyone's surprise, joined in the reunion and licked Rose as if she had been her own long-lost puppy:

> Then, of her own accord, she turned away, leaving Rose in possession, and took up a distant place on the foot of the bed, appealing to me with an almost human expression of mingled feelings — the heroic self-abnegation of new-born sympathy struggling with natural jealousy. The better feelings triumphed till both dogs fell asleep in their strangely reversed positions. On the next day she actually, for the first (and last) time in her life, made Rose welcome to a place beside her on the sacred shawl; where again they slept side by side. This however was the last gleam of the special sympathy called forth by Rose's troubles. From that day Fan decidedly and finally resumed her jealous occupation and guardianship of all sacred places and things, and maintained it energetically to her life's end.

Edward Jesse has written: 'A dog has been known to convey food to another of his species who was tied up and pining for want of it. A dog has frequently been seen to plunge involuntarily into a rapid stream to rescue another that was in danger of drowning.' As an example he tells of a man who was walking along a road in Lancashire 'when he was *accosted,* if the term may be used, by a terrier dog. The animal's gesticulations were at first so strange and unusual, that he felt inclined to get out of its way. The dog, however, at last by various significant signs and expressive looks, made his meaning known and the gentleman, to the dog's great delight, turned and followed him for a few hundred yards. He was led to the banks of a canal, which he had not before seen, and there he discovered a small dog struggling in the water for his life, and nearly exhausted by his efforts to save himself from drowning.' The man managed to pull the dog out, while the terrier watched intently, and Jesse concluded: 'It cannot be doubted, but that in this instance the terrier made use of the only means in his power to save the other dog, and this in a way which shewed a power of reasoning equally strong with that of a human being, under a similar circumstance.'

The grief that one dog can express for another is shown in the following excerpt from *In the Country,* and has a special value for me because it was written by my good friend the late Kenneth Allsop:

In the country
KENNETH ALLSOP
(1920–73)

I mentioned earlier how the Wessex air, pungent with the smell of badger and fox and rabbit, had galvanized my over-domesticated dachshunds — likewise the beagle, Galadriel, named (with ever more evident absurdity as her portliness increases) after the fairy queen in *Lord of the Rings.*

The trio began going AWOL on extended hunting forays. Mostly it was to the woods that they went and, as their earth-plastered coats showed, down into deep burrows, but they weren't always in pursuit of game. A nearby farmer's wife telephoned to ask — with admirable mildness — if we'd mind fetching our dogs, from whose jaws were being prised the dead hens. She demurred at being paid the value of the dead birds and had to be persuaded to accept the compensation. You can tell how good-hearted and understanding are my neighbours, but tolerance has its terminal point and I could not see how to be sure that another raid would not be committed.

I sentenced them to terms of being tethered. I raised my voice to a pitch where I frightened myself. I blocked every obvious bolt-hole, but with boundaries of shallow river and labyrinthine thicket there was no containing them. I shut them up in the old tennis court: a reasonable habitat for any but the most spoiled dogs, but you would have thought from their tremulous moans that they had been locked in a coal bunker.

After a lull, when I foolishly began to believe that they had reformed, they sneaked away again. They were missing two nights. Tilly, the dach bitch, and Gally turned up, exhausted and subdued. It was afternoon before we heard about Duffy, Tilly's four-year-old son.

His body had been found on a B-road three miles over the hill. There was no blood, no mutilation, so presumably it was only a glancing blow from a passing car, but it had killed him.

Duffy had unattractive traits. He was inclined to slyness. Under a disguise of innocence, he slunk. He was the one repeatedly to be discovered curled up in an armchair or the big saggy sofa in the sitting room, to which he tiptoed. Also, as became clear, he was the ringleader on those break-outs.

For since his death the other two do not go beyond the surrounding fields. Although some may scoff at such anthropomorphizing, it is not enough to say that they miss him: they mourn him.

They were good companions with an intricate three-direction relationship, and the sawn-off Duffy and the large, lolloping Gally, under whose belly he could walk without ducking, loved each other in male and female way.

With him gone, Gally and Tilly have changed. All these months later, their dejection makes his absence still tangible. They know where he is. We found them digging where we had buried him, so the stone was placed upon his grave.

We have also planted a rose there. Sentimental? I don't think so, for a family irrevocably alters when a member is lost, and it is well to keep remembrance. The flowers will feed upon his minerals and be brighter.

Rest in peace

I have sometimes thought of the final cause of dogs having such short lives and I am quite satisfied it is in compassion to the human race; for if we suffer so much in losing a dog after an acquaintance of ten or twelve years, what would it be if they were to live double that time?

SIR WALTER SCOTT
(1771–1832)

There are people who would regard an animal cemetery as morbid and even an epitaph to a dead dog as slightly absurd. They would not be owners of dogs themselves.

Many such memorials are delightful. There is the family graveyard in the gardens of Longleat, lines of stones in tribute to favourite pets:

Kestrel Kesty, found with broken wing. Lived 4 years; Green Parrott Jew Suss; even *Humbert's Woolly Monkey Johnny.* The gravestones to dogs go back as far as 1804: *St Bernard ROSE 4th Marquis of Bath;* to *Whippet DANNY 6th Marchioness of Bath 1940;* and *Shetland Sheepdog BRAN Lady Caroline Thynne 1941.*

A few miles from Hull, at a private house called Hotham Hall, there are several flat tombstones placed there by a professional soldier who served in the First World War and became so sickened by the waste of life that a signpost stands, incongruously, beside the gate today: 'To Ypres 347 Miles. In Defending the Salient Our Casualties were 90,000 killed; 71,000 missing; 410,000 wounded.' The horse that accompanied him to the war is honoured with this

76

inscription: 'To the memory of a Gallant Horse. Bred in Holderness and Hunted here. He landed in France 15 August 1914. Mons. Le Cateau. Cambre. He knew them all and Now Lies Here.'

This remarkable gentleman and officer honoured his dog as well:

Here lies my dog
Who crouched perhaps
Before some ghostly gate,
Awaits my step
As here he used to wait.

There is the more public cemetery in Hyde Park where Sir Henry Irving buried his terrier Fussie. There is no such person as the 'typical dog lover', and Irving, the sardonic ruler of the stage, was as soft as a young girl when it came to Fussie. Ellen Terry said that the actor loved his dog as much as his rehearsals, the highest praise she could think of, and described their mutual devotion: 'I have caught them often sitting opposite each other at Grafton Street just adoring each other! Occasionally Fussie would thump his tail on the ground to express his pleasure.' Originally, Fussie had belonged to her, with another terrier known as Charlie, but Irving won him over with a diet of 'chops, tomatoes, strawberries, asparagus, biscuits soaked in champagne', which sounds so undog-like, apart from the chops, that the actor must have used his magic as well. Once transferred, and the two became inseparable. Fussie travelled with him on his tours of America and if a hotel hinted that dogs were unwelcome, Irving left instantly. Fussie accompanied him to the theatre and once made a personal appearance at a charity performance after Irving had 'done his bit', as Ellen Terry related, and was putting on his hat and coat to leave. Assuming that the performance was over, Fussie bounded happily on stage in the middle of a mad scene, played by John Drew and Maude Adams in *A Pair of Lunatics*. As the actress gazed into the stage fire she heard Drew pause and exclaim:

Is this a dog I see before me
His tail towards my hand?

and wondered, for a moment, if he really had gone mad.

Appropriately, Fussie died on stage, in Manchester, where he scented a ham sandwich in a jacket which a stage-hand had thrown carelessly over the trap door. Fussie fell through the trap and was killed instantly. Later, Irving was found staring into space, hours on end, and the next day he carried the plump remains back to London and the Hyde Park cemetery where Fussie lies today.

The happiest animal cemetery I have visited lies on an island in the Seine, in the heart of Paris. There are paths and trees and gentle slopes, and the boats pass and hoot close by. A model of a whippet is overshadowed by a vast, rocklike sculpture inscribed with a crown and the declaration that the two pug-like dogs on top, wearing disconsolate, identical expressions carved in stone, belonged once to the 'Princess Lobanor'. But the inscription that touched me most, because it was so pathetically sincere, concerned a dog called Mopsik. I made this translation at the time:

> Our only friend. Mopsik 1926–38. Dear little Mopsik, so brave and affectionate, so faithful and so much truer than us who repaid the generosity of your tender, noble heart by having you killed! Because you were old and ill, you suffered, and we suffered with you. Dear Mopsik, forgive your ungrateful masters — their pain is infinite.

Mawkish perhaps, yet no less forlorn than those heartbreaking words on the graves of Flanders.

Sampy

JOHN EDWARDS

When I first read 'Sampy' in the *Daily Mail* I wrote to John Edwards and told him it should be in an anthology. Now it is.

As soon as the old man opened the door of the shed the parents came out bounding in the straw and she was lost underneath them in the tumble.

The mother had thick curly hair and the father was a big handsome dog with an important face. Border collies are like this.

The little one could hardly be seen at first. She had dust all over her, and a fat stomach that nearly touched the ground. Her face was white and black with some brown spots, and two blotches over the eyes that looked like small sunglasses pushed up on her forehead.

Her markings had sort of slipped to the right and when she came to me on those huge feet she was side-on and she never lost the habit.

I think she was the most beautiful thing I had ever seen. She could laugh and sometimes her face would look so sad you waited for the tears.

It was a quick deal. The man came down to £4 from £5 and she came home from Colchester lying on the floor under the driver's seat all of eight weeks old, and our lives were never going to be quite the same again.

She seemed to grow so quickly. Her legs got longer and longer and her feet got bigger and bigger and her face became so pretty they might have given her a screen test.

When she learned how to run she was low and fast. She could hunt sticks out of grass twice her height with her tail turning like a prop and the wind caught her fur and spread it like feathers.

We had settled for the name Scampy. Who knows why? It didn't make sense so we dropped the 'c' and then she was Sampy and it was a name no one had ever heard before.

Soon she was really part of everything that went on. No decision could be taken that did not include her.

We fell for that kind of silliness that goes with liking animals and nobody can explain it.

She walked every foot of Epping Forest, and the pools of the estuary and the banks that go by the canals in the Fens. She chased things that were only in her mind through seaweed in Maldon and when she got home she slept in a basket by the stove in the kitchen and sometimes her head and front paws were over the side and we sat and watched her for hours.

The first swim was in Pembrokeshire, in a deep, quiet pool on the corner of a wide stream. I think she fell in by accident through the rushes, and when the water came all around her she floated with her legs out.

The squeals were only in delight and we could never keep her from the water again.

She went with the boys across the beach at Picton and brought firewood back in her mouth. She came after gulls' eggs over the great cliffs at Ceibwr, and watched the lobsters coming out of the pots in the swirl of the sea off Tower Point.

She would lie still on the banks of the Cleddau when you cast a spinner over lazy trout, or follow a toad when it hopped to a hole, and then she would stand there with her head on one side and try to understand it.

She yapped at the fallen snow and rolled in it until she was covered and only her head could be seen, and then she would come wet to you and look where old towels hung and wait to be dried.

Her best position in the field was at deep extra cover, and she would snap a ball out of the air and bring it to the wicket. In football she would have been a full back because nobody dribbled past her.

Once, the Queen turned her head down to see her in Windsor Park, sitting smart on a hedge by the Long Walk.

There were plenty of suitors. There was Choco at first, and then Big Paws and Simon, Jinx, Sandy (she liked him best of all), Kim, William and Tommy Evans's dog. She was never actually married.

She linked the years between our real youth and whatever you call it now. She was there in all the big times. Her eyes were brown in the middle surrounded by a deep, cloudy blue, and her coat shone like wet slate.

Then she wanted to do a little less work. Not quite as far through the park. Not quite as high over Watlington Hill. Not too much swimming either. Just a little bit. When it was very warm.

There was grey now on her face and her old feet splayed a bit. In age she became even more beautiful. That morning by Smiths Lawn, rolling through the ferns with cobwebs and dewdrops sticking on her, and then at the end a pink tongue just hanging from her mouth and a smile for the picture that was never taken.

Much slower now. Much, much slower, Just a walk. No running. No sticks to be thrown, thank you. I've done all that. And Iris would take her just over the fields for a bit, but sleeping was now Sampy's favourite thing.

It was last week that we all knew. She was in a stream under Mynydd Bach with the water just over her feet and she looked around and her eyes were foggy and it had all gone from her.

There was no strength any more. No muscled legs and pumping heart and lungs full of breath to carry her anywhere. She came home from Wales in my arms and she couldn't lift her head to say goodbye.

It wasn't a day we want to remember. Lightning splattered in the sky and the thunder exploded everywhere. Sampy hated thunder.

She was lying on the couch, just a very tired old lady with all her life over.

It's almost always the same. The vet cuts a little bit of hair from the foreleg and puts a needle in with a huge dose of chloroform. She was one hundred. The eyes never fully close.

She was gone in about a second and part of our life went with her.

A Field Marshal on the subject of dogs

Like many of our military leaders, Field Marshal Wavell had an artistic side to his nature which he expressed in his delightful anthology of poetry *Other Men's Flowers*. But I cannot agree that 'The dog, man's most intelligent and responsive friend in the animal world, has inspired little real poetry, while that foolish quadruped the horse has been the subject of much. Beauty and speed have nearly always been preferred to solid worth — this is the reason for many divorces.'

He continues: 'The truth is that the dog-friend is too sensible, too homely to appeal to the poet, by whom even the sleek, egotistical promiscuous cat is better advertised. Poor dog, his name is ill connected in our speech: a dog's life, sick as a dog, dog's eared, dog tired, dogsbody. And why should the name of the dog's comparatively chaste female be such a term of opprobrium while the cat's noisier and more frequent lapses from virtue escape notice? Perhaps merely because the cat is a nocturnal amorist, while the dog, sensibly, likes to see what he is making love to — not that he seems to mind much.

'Never mind, dogs have their star and cats have none.'

I hope the poems included here, by Southey, Byron and Wordsworth, refute his suggestion that dogs have inspired 'little real poetry'.

There are many noble memorials to dogs. I have been brash enough to adapt, loosely, the words of a famous Greek epitaph on a stone beside some former roadway:

> You who pass this way
> And see this monument,
> Laugh not I pray,
> For though this is a testament
> To dog, tears fell for me
> And earth above was turned
> By man who writes these words
> In fondest memory.

Upon his Spaniel Tracye

Now thou art dead, no eye shall ever see,
For shape and service Spaniel like to thee.

This shall my love do, give thy sad death one
Tear, that deserves of me a million.
ROBERT HERRICK
(1591–1674)
from *Hesperides,* 1648

On the Death of a Favourite Old Spaniel

And they have drown'd thee then at last! poor Phillis!
The burden of old age was heavy on thee,
And yet thou should'st have lived! What though thine eye
Was dim, and watch'd no more with eager joy
The wonted call that on thy dull sense sunk
With fruitless repetition, the warm Sun
Might still have cheer'd thy slumbers; thou did'st love
To lick the hand that fed thee, and though past
Youth's active season, even Life itself
Was comfort. Poor old friend, how earnestly
Would I have pleaded for thee! thou had'st been
Still the companion of my boyish sports;
And as I roam'd o'er Avon's woody cliffs,
From many a day dream has thy short quick bark
Recall'd my wandering soul. I have beguiled
Often the melancholy hours at school,
Sour'd by some little tyrant, with the thought
Of distant home, and I remember'd then
Thy faithful fondness; for not mean the joy
Returning at the happy holydays,
I felt from thy dumb welcome. Pensively
Sometimes have I remark'd thy slow decay,
Feeling myself changed too, and musing much
On many a sad vicissitude of Life.
Ah poor companion! When thou followed'st last
Thy master's footsteps to the gate
Which closed for ever on him, thou did'st lose
Thy truest friend and none was left to plead
For the old age of brute fidelity.
But fare thee well! Mine is no narrow creed;
And He who gave thee being did not frame
The mystery of life to be the sport
Of merciless Man. There is another world
For all that live and move . . . a better one!
Where the proud bipeds who would fain confine
INFINITE GOODNESS to the little bounds
Of their own charity, may envy thee!
ROBERT SOUTHEY
(1774–1843)

83

It is remarkable that Robert Southey should have written these lines when he was only twenty-two, not because they are so confident but because they are so perceptive and understanding of 'the old age of brute fidelity'. Not for him the easy alibi 'it's for the dog's sake', nor the discourtesy of introducing a puppy into the house so that it can take over when the old dog has had his day.

Lord Byron wrote this poem in 1808 when he was twenty:

Inscription on the Monument of a Newfoundland Dog

When some proud son of man returns to earth,
Unknown to glory, but upheld by birth,
The sculptor's art exhausts the pomp of woe,
And storied urns record who rest below:
When all is done, upon the tomb is seen,
Not what he was, but what he should have been:
But the poor dog, in life the firmest friend,
The first to welcome, foremost to defend,
Whose honest heart is still his master's own,
Who labours, fights, lives, breathes for him alone,
Unhonour'd falls, unnoticed all his worth,
Denied in heaven the soul he held on earth,
While man, vain insect! hopes to be forgiven,
And claims himself a sole exclusive heaven.
Oh man! thou feeble tenant of an hour,
Debased by slavery, or corrupt by power,
Who knows thee well, must quit thee with disgust,
Degraded mass of animated dust!
Thy love is lust, thy friendship all a cheat,
Thy smiles hypocrisy, thy words deceit!
By nature vile, ennobled but by name,
Each kindred brute might bid thee blush for shame.
Ye! who perchance behold this simple urn,
Pass on — it honours none you wish to mourn:
To mark a friend's remains these stones arise;
I never knew but one — and here he lies.
LORD BYRON
(1788–1824)

Few dogs would join in such a harsh verdict on mankind! But surely this must rank as one of the most magnificent of tributes to any dog: 'The first to welcome, foremost to defend.' That tells it all.

There is another tribute from a great poet, written by William Wordsworth when he was thirty-five and living at Grasmere.

84

Tribute

Lie here, without a record of thy worth,
Beneath a covering of the common earth!
It is not from unwillingness to praise,
Or want of love, that here no Stone we raise;
More thou deserv'st; but *this* man gives to man,
Brother to brother, *this* is all we can.
Yet they to whom thy virtues made thee dear
Shall find thee through all changes of the year:
This Oak points out thy grave; the silent tree
Will gladly stand a monument of thee.
We grieved for thee, and wished thy end were past;
And willingly have laid thee here at last:
For thou hadst lived till everything that cheers
In thee had yielded to the weight of years;
Extreme old age had wasted thee away,
And left thee but a glimmering of the day;
Thy ears were deaf, and feeble were thy knees —
I saw thee stagger in the summer breeze,
Too weak to stand against its sportive breath,
And ready for the gentlest stroke of death.
It came, and we were glad; yet tears were shed;
Both man and woman wept when thou wert dead;
Not only for a thousand thoughts that were,
Old household thoughts, in which thou hadst thy share;
But for some precious boons vouchsafed to thee,
Found scarcely anywhere in like degree!
For love, that comes wherever life and sense
Are given by God, in thee was most intense;
A chain of heart, a feeling of the mind,
A tender sympathy, which did thee bind
Not only to us Men, but to thy Kind:
Yea, for thy fellow-brutes in thee we saw
A soul of love, love's intellectual law:—
Hence, if we wept, it was not done in shame;
Our tears from passion and from reason came
And, therefore, shalt thou be an honoured name!
WILLIAM WORDSWORTH
(1770–1850)

Argus greets Ulysses

Thus, near the gates conferring as they drew,
Argus the dog, his ancient master knew:
He not unconscious of the voice and tread,
Lifts to the sound his ear, and rears his head;
Bred by Ulysses, nourished at his board,
But, ah! not fated long to please his lord;

To him, his sweetness and his strength were vain;
The voice of glory call'd him o'er the main.
Till then in every sylvan chase renown'd,
With Argus, Argus, rang the woods around;
With him the youth pursued the goat or fawn,
Or traced the mazy leveret o'er the lawn.
Now left to man's ingratitude he lay,
Unhoused, neglected in the public way.

He knew his lord; he knew, and strove to meet:
In vain he strove to crawl, and kiss his feet;
Yet (all he could) his tail, his ears, his eyes,
Salute his master, and confess his joys.
Soft pity touch'd the mighty master's soul;
Adown his cheek a tear unbidden stole.

The dog, whom Fate had granted to behold
His lord, when twenty tedious years had roll'd,
Takes a last look, and, having seen him, dies;
So closed forever faithful Argus' eyes!
HOMER
from *The Odyssey* (Book XVII)
translated by Pope

Gough and his Dog – (an extract)

Sir Walter Scott's account of a dog whose master fell down a
precipice in a fog on Helvellyn in Cumberland in 1805 and was
dashed to pieces.

Dark green was the spot, 'mid the brown mountain heather,
    Where the pilgrim of nature lay stretched in decay;
Like the corpse of an outcast, abandoned to weather,
    Till the mountain winds wasted the tenantless clay:
Nor yet quite deserted, though lonely extended,
    For faithful in death his mute favourite attended,
The much loved remains of his master defended,
    And chased the hill fox and the raven away.
SIR WALTER SCOTT

Loyalty to memory

Soon we were on our way out from the pool, my back to the Island of my birth and my face to the mainland. I heard barking behind me. I knew well what it was. Looking back I saw Rose out on the bank howling as she saw me departing from her. I crushed down the distress that was putting a cloud upon my heart.

MAURICE O'SULLIVAN
from *Twenty Years A-growing*

A man's grief for his dog is no less than the dog's for him. The animal is devastated because so much that he has understood has gone. His grief has nothing to do with rank or wealth. If his diet has been sirloin served by a millionaire, or scraps shared by a tramp, it is probable that the latter will have won the greater loyalty.

The familiar story of the Dog of Aughrim is recorded by Edward Jesse:

> At the hard-fought battle of Aughrim, an Irish officer was accompanied by his wolf hound. This gentleman was killed and stript in the battle, but the dog remained by his body both by day and night. He fed upon some of the other bodies with the rest of the dogs, yet he would not allow them or anything else to touch that of his master. When all the other bodies were consumed, the other dogs departed, but this used to go in the night to the adjacent villages for food, and presently to return again to the place where his master's bones were only then left. This he continued to do from July, when the battle was fought, 'till the January following, when a soldier being quartered near, and going that way by chance, the dog, fearing he came to disturb his master's bones, flew upon the soldier, who, being surprised at the suddenness of the thing, unslung his carbine, he having been thrown on his back, and killed the noble animal. He expired with the same fidelity to the remains of his unfortunate master, as that master had shewn devotion to the cause of his unhappy country.

This reminds me of an explanation I was given for the name of 'The Isle of Dogs' in the East End of London. There are several versions: it was once so forlorn and empty, lined with gibbets, that returning sailors felt it was a place that 'had gone to the dogs'. More convincingly it is claimed that when King Charles stayed at Greenwich Palace he kept his spaniels on the marshland opposite so that their barking would not disturb him. But the following explanation is my favourite: that a waterman was murdered by a colleague who fled across the water while the dead man's dog stayed faithfully beside his master's corpse. At last, desperate with hunger, the dog swam across to Greenwich at low tide and was fed by other watermen who recognized him. After several journeys, the dog suddenly cornered one particular waterman with such ferocity that the man confessed to the murder. There is only one snag: surely the place would have been called Dog Island in the singular, and not the Isle of Dogs? I am reluctant to point this out and spoil the story.

Greyfriar's Bobby is probably the best documented case of all. Bobby belonged to a Midlothian farmer called Gray, in the middle of the last century. Every Wednesday Gray came to Edinburgh for market day, with his shaggy terrier Bobby. They lunched at Traill's, a modest restaurant in Greyfriars, and Bobby's treat was a handsome bun.

Gray died in 1858 and was buried in Greyfriars Churchyard. Three days later Mr Traill was startled to see Bobby come into the room, woebegone and plainly hungry, a pitiful contrast to the once-loved dog. The man handed the customary bun to Bobby who ran off with it in his mouth. After several such visits, Traill followed the dog and saw him eating his meal on his master's grave. It seemed that Bobby had been the only mourner, or at least the only mourner to stay. Neighbours heard of this and brought him to their homes but every attempt was followed by escape. The mound of earth in the graveyard was the only place he was prepared to accept. There was a sign on the gate, 'Dogs not admitted', but James Brown, the keeper, made Bobby the exception. And so Bobby stayed there for the rest of his life, apart from excursions for buns — all other offers were refused. In bad winter weather he crouched under a tombstone, until they built a special shelter for him near the grave. In spite of this uncomfortable existence, Bobby lived to a great age, for a further fourteen years, and was finally buried in the same churchyard near his master. There can be little doubt that this is what he would have wished, and perhaps had wished for all along.

Even this proof of devotion is not unique. In the severe winter of 1953–4, an elderly shepherd called Joseph Tagg set out for a walk with his dog Tip and suffered from a heart attack on the Derbyshire moors. The man died, but Tip stayed by his master as the heavy snowstorm on the night of 12th December gradually covered their bodies. When the search party found them in the spring when the snow had melted, Tip was still there though barely alive. He died

soon afterwards from starvation and exposure and a memorial stands in tribute on Howden Moor:

> IN COMMEMORATION OF TIP, the sheepdog which stayed by the body of her dead master, Mr Joseph Tagg, on the Howden Moors for fifteen weeks from 12th December 1953 to 27th March 1954. Erected by public subscription.

The working dog

The working dog confounds every animal with his versatility. The horse provides transport, but the majority of animals — in our general arrogance that they are put there for our benefit — are used for skins or food.

Fortunately, dogs are not eaten, except in the Far East where they have been regarded as a delicacy. Not so long ago there was a report in *The Times* of an American couple who visited a restaurant, in Hong Kong, with their pet poodle. They gestured to the waiter that they wanted something for the dog to eat and he was led into the kitchen. They ordered their own meal and waited. After a long delay they asked for their dog, but at this moment the smiling waiter reappeared bearing a tray with a large silver dish which revealed, when the lid was removed, their braised poodle set among bamboo shoots. The waiter could not understand the commotion, but the Americans flew back to New York that night in a state of understandable shock.

The working dog takes many forms: among the most remarkable are the Seeing-Eye dogs for the blind. I spoke to a blind man who told me that the arrival of 'Archie' had changed his life completely. At last he was independent, and after the initial training he could tell the dog, 'office' or 'pub' and leave together without having to ask a member of his family. Apparently Archie knew that he was blind, carefully moving out of his way when the telephone rang while he let other members of the family step over or around him in order to answer it. All Seeing Eye dogs, usually labradors, are retired when they reach the age of ten. Then they are returned to the training college, or they can be kept. 'Of course there is no question,' the blind man told me, 'Archie will have given me the best years of his life and will end his days being looked after himself, at home.'

The Eskimo dog is the horse of the north, providing transport and possessing exceptional strength — seven can run a mile in four minutes drawing a heavy sledge full of men. They seem immune to cold.

In the countryside, the web-footed Otterhound is extinct, like other breeds exploited by man in his pursuit of wild life, though some, like the Dachshund, the German badger hound, have become domesticated.

The greyhound is another dog taught to race and kill hares, but, like the foxhound, is less to blame than the soldier who obeys his officer. The bulldog was used originally in the so-called sport of bull-baiting, but has now become a happier symbol of tenacity.

The most constant of working dogs is surely the sheepdog, vigilant, patient, and dutiful. The indispensable companion of the shepherd.

The shepherd's dog
EDWARD JESSE

Robert Murray, Shepherd to Mr Samuel Richmond, Path of Coudie, near Dunning in Perthshire, had purchased for his master four score of sheep at the Falkirk Tryst, but having occasion to stop another day, and confident in the faithfulness and sagacity of his Collie, which was a female, he committed the drove to her care, with orders to drive them home, a distance of about seventeen miles. The poor animal, when a few miles on the road, dropped two whelps, but faithful to her charge, she drove the sheep on a mile or two further, then, allowing them to stop, returned for her pups, which she carried for about two miles in advance of the sheep. Leaving her pups, the Collie again returned for the sheep, and drove them onwards a few miles. This she continued to do, alternately carrying her own young ones and taking charge of the flock, till she reached home. The manner of her acting, on this occasion, was afterwards gathered by the Shepherd from various individuals, who had observed these extraordinary proceedings of the dumb animal on the road. However, when the Collie reached her home, and delivered her charge, it was found that the two pups were dead. In this extremity, the instinct of the poor brute was, if possible, still more remarkable. She went to a rabbit brae in the vicinity, and dug out of the earth two young rabbits, which she deposited on some straw in a barn, and continued to suckle for some time, until one of the farm servants unluckily let down a full sack upon them and smothered them.

Wully, the story of a Yaller Dog

ERNEST SETON-THOMPSON
(1860–1946)

Curiously neglected today, the American writer Ernest Seton-Thompson was one of the greatest tellers of animal stories, with 'Wully, the story of a Yaller Dog' as a prime example. This was included in *Wild Animals I Have Known,* published in 1898.

Later, rather oddly, he reversed his name to Ernest Thompson Seton and made his home in Seton Village, Santa Fe, New Mexico. He founded the Woodcraft Indians, a precursor of the Boy Scout Movement, and died at the age of eighty-six in 1946.

Away up in the Cheviots little Wully was born. He and one other of the litter were kept; his brother because he resembled the best dog in the vicinity, and himself because he was a little yellow beauty.

His early life was that of a sheep-dog, in company with an experienced collie who trained him, and an old shepherd who was scarcely inferior to them in intelligence. By the time he was two years old Wully was full grown and had taken a thorough course in sheep. He knew them from ram-horn to lamb-hoof, and old Robin, his master, at length had such confidence in his sagacity that he would frequently stay at the tavern all night while Wully guarded the woolly idiots in the hills. His education had been wisely bestowed and in most ways he was a very bright little dog with a future before him. Yet he never learned to despise that addle-pated Robin. The old shepherd, with all his faults, his continual striving after his ideal state — intoxication — and his mind-shrivelling life in general was rarely brutal to Wully, and Wully repaid him with an exaggerated worship that the greatest and wisest in the land would have aspired to in vain.

Wully could not have imagined any greater being than Robin, and yet for the sum of five shillings a week all Robin's vital energy and mental force were pledged to the service of a not very great cattle and sheep dealer, the real proprietor of Wully's charge, and when this man, really less great than the neighbouring laird, ordered Robin to drive his flock by stages to the Yorkshire moors and markets, of all the 376 mentalities concerned, Wully's was the most interested and interesting.

The journey through Northumberland was uneventful. At the River Tyne the sheep were driven on to the ferry and landed safely in smoky South Shields. The great factory chimneys were just starting up for the day and belching out fogbanks and thunder-rollers of opaque leaden smoke that darkened the air and hung low like a storm-cloud over the streets. The sheep thought that they recognized the fuming dun of an unusually heavy Cheviot storm. They became alarmed, and in spite of their keepers stampeded through the town in 374 different directions.

Robin was vexed to the inmost recesses of his tiny soul. He stared stupidly after the sheep for half a minute, then gave the order, 'Wully, fetch them in.' After this mental effort he sat down, lit his pipe, and taking out his knitting began work on a half-finished sock.

To Wully the voice of Robin was the voice of God. Away he ran in 374 different directions, and headed off and rounded up the 374 different wanderers, and brought them back to the ferry-house before Robin, who was stolidly watching the process, had toed off his sock.

Finally Wully — not Robin — gave the sign that all were in. The old shepherd proceeded to count them — 370, 371, 372, 373.

'Wully,' he said reproachfully, 'thar no' a' here. Thur's anither.' And Wully, stung with shame, bounded off to scout the whole city for the missing one. He was not long gone when a small boy pointed out to Robin that the sheep were all there, the whole 374. Now Robin was in a quandary. His order was to hasten on to Yorkshire, and yet he knew that Wully's pride would prevent his coming back without another sheep, even if he had to steal it. Such things had happened before, and resulted in embarrassing complications. What should he do? There was five shillings a week at stake. Wully was a good dog, it was a pity to lose him, but then, his orders from the master; and again, if Wully stole an extra sheep to make up the number, then what — in a foreign land too? He decided to abandon Wully, and push on alone with the sheep. And how he fared no one knows or cares.

Meanwhile, Wully careered through miles of streets hunting in vain for his lost sheep. All day he searched, and at night, famished and worn out, he sneaked shamefacedly back to the ferry, only to find that master and sheep had gone. His sorrow was pitiful to see. He ran about whimpering, then took the ferryboat across to the other side, and searched everywhere for Robin. He returned to South Shields and searched there, and spent the rest of the night seeking for his wretched idol. The next day he continued his search, he crossed and recrossed the river many times. He watched and smelt everyone that came over, and with significant shrewdness he sought unceasingly in the neighbouring taverns for his master. The next day he set to work systematically to smell everyone that might cross the ferry.

The ferry makes fifty trips a day, with an average of one hundred persons a trip, yet never once did Wully fail to be on the gang-plank and smell every pair of legs that crossed — 5,000 pairs, 10,000 legs that day did Wully examine after his own fashion. And the next day, and the next, and all the next week he kept his post, and seemed indifferent to feeding himself. Soon starvation and worry began to tell on him. He grew thin and ill-tempered. No one could touch him, and any attempt to interfere with his daily occupation of leg-smelling roused him to desperation.

Day after day, week after week Wully watched and waited for his master, who never came. The ferry men learned to respect Wully's fidelity. At first he scorned their proffered food and shelter, and lived no one knew how, but starved to it at last, he accepted the gifts and learned to tolerate the givers. Although embittered against the world, his heart was true to his worthless master.

Fourteen months afterward I made his acquaintance. He was still on rigid duty at his post. He had regained his good looks. His bright, keen face set off by his white ruff and pricked ears made a dog to catch the eye anywhere. But he gave me no second glance, once he found my legs were not those he sought, and in spite of my friendly overtures during the ten months following that he continued his watch, I got no farther into his confidence than any other stranger.

For two whole years did this devoted creature attend that ferry. There was only one thing to prevent him going home to the hills, not the distance nor the chance of getting lost, but the conviction that Robin, the godlike Robin, wished him to stay by the ferry; and he stayed.

But he crossed the water as often as he felt it would serve his purpose. The fare for a dog was one penny, and it was calculated that Wully owed the company hundreds of pounds before he gave up his quest. He never failed to sense every pair of nethers that crossed the gangplank — 6,000,000 legs by computation had been pronounced upon by this expert. But all to no purpose. His unswerving fidelity never faltered, though his temper was obviously souring under the long strain.

We had never heard what became of Robin, but one day a sturdy drover strode down the ferry-slip and Wully mechanically assaying the new personality, suddenly started, his mane bristled, he trembled, a low growl escaped him, and he fixed his every sense on the drover.

One of the ferry hands not understanding, called to the stranger, 'Hoot mon, ye maunna hort oor dawg.'

'Whaes hortin 'im, ye fule; he is mair like to hort me.' But further explanation was not necessary. Wully's manner had wholly changed. He fawned on the drover, and his tail was wagging violently for the first time in years.

A few words made it all clear. Dorley, the drover, had known Robin very well, and the mittens and comforter he wore were of Robin's own make and had once been part of his wardrobe. Wully recognized the traces of his master, and despairing of any nearer approach to his lost idol, he abandoned his post at the ferry and plainly announced his intention of sticking to the owner of the mittens, and Dorley was well-pleased to take Wully along to his home among the hills of Derbyshire, where he became once more a sheep-dog in charge of a flock.

Monsaldale is one of the best-known valleys in Derbyshire. The Pig and Whistle is its single but celebrated inn, and Jo Greatorex, the landlord, is a shrewd and sturdy Yorkshireman. Nature meant him for a frontiersman, but circumstances made him an innkeeper and his inborn tastes made him a — well, never mind; there was a great deal of poaching done in that country.

Wully's new home was on the upland east of the valley above Jo's inn, and the fact was not without weight in bringing me to Monsaldale. His master, Dorley, farmed in a small way on the lowland, and on the moors had a large number of sheep. These Wully guarded with his old-time sagacity, watching them while they fed and bringing them to the fold at night. He was reserved and preoccupied for a dog, and rather too ready to show his teeth to strangers, but he was so unremitting in his attention to his flock that Dorley did not lose a lamb that year, although the neighbouring farmers paid the usual tribute to eagles and to foxes.

The dales are poor fox-hunting country at best. The rocky ridges, high stone walls, and precipices are too numerous to please the riders, and the final retreats in the rocks are so plentiful that it was a marvel the foxes did not overrun Monsaldale. But they didn't. There had been but little reason for complaint until the year 1881, when a sly old fox quartered himself on the fat parish, like a mouse inside a cheese, and laughed equally at the hounds of the huntsmen and the lurchers of the farmers.

He was several times run by the Peak hounds and escaped by making for the Devil's Hole. Once in this gorge, where the cracks in the rocks extend unknown distances, he was safe. The country folk began to see something more than chance in the fact that he always escaped at the Devil's Hole, and when one of the hounds who nearly caught this Devil's Fox soon after went mad, it removed all doubt as to the spiritual paternity of said fox.

He continued his career of rapine, making audacious raids and hair-breadth escapes, and finally began, as do many old foxes, to kill from a mania for slaughter. Thus it was that Digby lost ten lambs in one night. Carroll lost seven the next night. Later, the vicarage duck-pond was wholly devastated, and scarcely a night passed but someone in the region had to report a carnage of poultry, lambs or sheep, and, finally even calves.

Of course all the slaughter was attributed to this one fox of the Devil's Hole. It was known only that he was a very large fox, at least one that made a very large track. He never was clearly seen, even by the huntsmen. And it was noticed that Thunder and Bell, the stanchest hounds in the pack, had refused to tongue or even to follow the trail when he was hunted.

His reputation for madness sufficed to make the master of the Peak hounds avoid the neighbourhood. The farmers in Monsaldale, led by Jo, agreed among themselves that if it would only come on a snow, they would assemble and beat the whole country, and in defiance of all rules of the hunt, get rid of the 'daft' fox in any way they could. But the snow did not come, and the red-haired gentleman lived his life. Notwithstanding his madness, he did not lack method. He never came two successive nights to the same farm. He never ate where he killed, and he never left a track that betrayed his retreat. He usually finished up his night's trail on the turf, or on a public highway.

Once I saw him. I was walking to Monsaldale from Bakewell late one night during a heavy storm, and as I turned the corner of Stead's sheep-fold there was a vivid flash of lightning. By its light, there was fixed on my retina a picture that made me start. Sitting on his haunches by the roadside, twenty yards away, was a very large fox gazing at me with malignant eyes, and licking his muzzle in a suggestive manner. All this I saw, but no more, and might have forgotten it, or thought myself mistaken, but the next morning, in that very fold, were found the bodies of twenty-three lambs and sheep, and the unmistakable signs that brought home the crime to the well-known marauder.

There was only one man who escaped, and that was Dorley. This was the more remarkable because he lived in the centre of the region raided, and within one mile of the Devil's Hole. Faithful Wully proved himself worth all the dogs in the neighbourhood. Night after night he brought in the sheep, and never one was missing. The Mad Fox might prowl about the Dorley homestead if he wished, but Wully, shrewd, brave, active Wully was more than a match for him, and not only saved his master's flock, but himself escaped with a whole skin. Everyone entertained a profound respect for him, and he might have been a popular pet but for his temper which, never genial, became more and more crabbed. He seemed to like Dorley, and Huldah, Dorley's eldest daughter, a shrewd, handsome, young woman, who, in the capacity of general manager of the house, was Wully's special guardian. The other members of Dorley's family Wully learned to tolerate, but the rest of the world, men and dogs, he seemed to hate.

His uncanny disposition was well shown in the last meeting I had with him. I was walking on a pathway across the moor behind Dorley's house. Wully was lying on the doorstep. As I drew near he arose, and without appearing to see me trotted towards my pathway and placed himself across it about ten yards ahead of me. There he stood silently and intently regarding the distant moor, his slightly bristling mane the only sign that he had not been suddenly turned to stone. He did not stir as I came up, and not wishing to quarrel, I stepped around past his nose and walked on. Wully at once left his position and in the same eerie silence trotted on some twenty feet and again stood across the pathway. Once more I came up and, stepping into the grass, brushed past his nose. Instantly, but without a sound, he seized my left heel, I kicked out with the other foot, but he escaped. Not having a stick, I flung a large stone at him. He leaped forward and the stone struck him in the ham, bowling him over into a ditch. He gasped out a savage growl as he fell, but scrambled out of the ditch and limped away in silence.

Yet sullen and ferocious as Wully was to the world, he was always gentle with Dorley's sheep. Many were the tales of rescues told of him. Many a poor lamb that had fallen into a pond or hole would have perished but for his timely and sagacious aid, many a far-weltered ewe did he turn right side up; while his keen eye discerned and his fierce courage baffled every eagle that had appeared on the moor in his time.

The Monsaldale farmers were still paying their nightly tribute to the Mad Fox, when the snow came, late in December. Poor Widow Gelt lost her entire flock of twenty sheep, and the fiery cross went forth early in the morning. With guns unconcealed the burly farmers set out to follow to the finish the tell-tale tracks in the snow, those of a very large fox, undoubtedly the multo-murderous villain. For awhile the trail was clear enough, then it came to the river and the habitual cunning of the animal was shown. He reached the water at a long angle pointing down stream and jumped into the shallow, unfrozen current. But at the other side there was no track leading out, and it was only after long searching that, a quarter of a mile higher up the stream, they found where he had come out. The track then ran to the top of Henley's high stone wall, where there was no snow left to tell tales. But the patient hunters persevered. When it crossed the smooth snow from the wall to the high road there was a difference of opinion. Some claimed that the track went up, others down the road. But Jo settled it, and after another long search they found where apparently the same trail, though some said a larger one had left the road to enter a sheep-fold, and leaving this without harming the occupants, the track-maker had stepped in the footmarks of a countryman, thereby getting to the moor road, along which he had trotted straight to Dorley's farm.

That day the sheep were kept in on account of the snow and Wully, without his usual occupation, was lying on some planks in the sun. As the hunters drew near the house, he growled savagely and sneaked around to where the sheep were. Jo Greatorex walked up to where Wully had crossed the fresh snow, gave a glance, looked dumbfounded, then pointing to the retreating sheep-dog, he said, with emphasis:

'Lads, we're off the track of the Fox. But there's the killer of the Widder's yowes.'

Some agreed with Jo, others recalled the doubt in the trail and were for going back to make a fresh follow. At this juncture, Dorley himself came out of the house.

'Tom,' said Jo, 'that dog o' thine 'as killed twenty of Widder

Gelt's sheep, last night. An' ah fur one don't believe as its 'is first killin'.'

'Why, mon, thou art crazy,' said Tom, 'Ah never 'ad a better sheep-dog — 'e fair loves the sheep.'

'Aye! We's seen summat o' that in las' night's work,' replied Jo.

In vain the company related the history of the morning. Tom swore that it was nothing but a jealous conspiracy to rob him of Wully.

'Wully sleeps i' the kitchen every night. Never is oot till he's let to bide wi' the yowes. Why, mon, he's wi' oor sheep the year round, and never a hoof have ah lost.'

Tom became much excited over this abominable attempt against Wully's reputation and life. Jo and his partisans got equally angry, and it was a wise suggestion of Huldah's that quieted them.

'Feyther,' said she, 'ah'll sleep i' the kitchen the night. If Wully 'as ae way of gettin' oot ah'll see it, an' if he's no oot an' sheep's killed on the country-side, we'll ha' proof it's na Wully.'

That night Huldah stretched herself on the settee and Wully slept as usual underneath the table. As night wore on the dog became restless. He turned on his bed and once or twice got up, stretched, looked at Huldah and lay down again. About two o'clock he seemed no longer able to resist some strange impulse. He arose quietly, looked toward the low window, then at the motionless girl. Huldah lay still and breathed as though sleeping. Wully slowly came near and sniffed and breathed his doggy breath in her face. She made no move. He nudged her gently with his nose. Then, with his sharp ears forward and his head on one side he studied her calm face. Still no sign. He walked quietly to the window, mounted the table without noise, placed his nose under the sash-bar and raised the light frame until he could put one paw underneath. Then changing, he put his nose under the sash and raised it high enough to slip out, easing down the frame finally on his rump and tail with an adroitness that told of long practice. Then he disappeared into the darkness.

From her couch Huldah watched in amazement. After waiting for some time to make sure that he was gone, she arose, intending to call her father at once, but on second thought she decided to await more conclusive proof. She peered into the darkness, but no sign of Wully was to be seen. She put more wood on the fire, and lay down again. For over an hour she lay wide awake listening to the kitchen clock, and starting at each trifling sound, and wondering

101

what the dog was doing. Could it be possible that he had really killed the widow's sheep? Then the recollection of his gentleness to their own sheep came, and completed her perplexity.

Another hour slowly tick-tocked. She heard a slight sound at the window that made her heart jump. The scratching sound was soon followed by the lifting of the sash, and in a short time Wully was back in the kitchen with the window closed behind him.

By the flickering fire-light Huldah could see a strange, wild gleam in his eye, and his jaws and snowy breast were dashed with fresh blood. The dog ceased his slight panting as he scrutinized the girl. Then, as she did not move, he lay down, and began to lick his paws and muzzle, growling lowly once or twice as though at the remembrance of some recent occurrence.

Huldah had seen enough. There could no longer be any doubt that Jo was right and more — a new thought flashed into her quick brain, she realized that the weird fox of Monsal was before her. Raising herself, she looked straight at Wully, and exclaimed:

'Wully! Wully! so it's a' true — oh, Wully, ye terrible brute.'

Her voice was fiercely reproachful, it rang in the quiet kitchen, and Wully recoiled as though shot. He gave a desperate glance toward the closed window. His eye gleamed, and his mane bristled. But he cowered under her gaze, and grovelled on the floor as though begging for mercy. Slowly he crawled nearer and nearer, as if to lick her feet, until quite close, then, with the fury of a tiger, but without a sound, he sprang for her throat.

The girl was taken unawares, but she threw up her arm in time, and Wully's long, gleaming tusks sank into her flesh, and grated on the bone.

'Help! help! feyther! feyther!' she shrieked.

Wully was a light weight, and for a moment she flung him off. But there could be no mistaking his purpose. The game was up, it was his life or hers now.

'Feyther! feyther!' she screamed, as the yellow fury, striving to kill her, bit and tore the unprotected hands that had so often fed him.

In vain she fought to hold him off, he would soon have had her by the throat, when in rushed Dorley.

Straight at him, now in the same horrid silence sprang Wully, and savagely tore him again and again before a deadly blow from the fagot-hook disabled him, dashing him, gasping and writhing, on the stone floor, desperate and done for, but game and defiant to

102

the last. Another quick blow scattered his brains on the hearthstone, where so long he had been a faithful and honoured retainer — and Wully, bright, fierce, trusty, treacherous Wully, quivered a moment, then straightened out, and lay forever still.

Faithful unto death

When dog days are over

Bassey is a grand old dog. Her cheerful, black-and-white clown's face is scarred now from plunging into brambles after rabbits; her eyes water, and the fur has been worn down around them; her tail usually sports a bloodstain where she has been scratched by a thorn. She looks as if she has just emerged from a fight.

And so, in a way, she has. On the sand dunes last summer she was bitten by an adder in the throat, so painfully that she howled through the night even though the vet had given her an injection. I have never heard a dog make such human sounds, as if she was crying out: 'Oh *no!* I can't bear it!'

I did my best to hold and comfort her until, at dawn, she was violently, thankfully sick. After she coughed up an awful flow of yellow, she sank down exhausted and slept. When she woke up she had regained her old, slightly foolish contentment.

But a few months ago she had to have an operation to remove an infected womb. She was kept at the vet's surgery over the weekend and for two days it was doubtful if she would come back. But she did — and started hunting again.

It was too good to last — she had to go in again for a further operation. When the faithful vet brought her back, the same evening this time, she padded into the house with a glassy glance of despair and headed straight for the cupboard in the corner of my bedroom, where she likes to disappear.

She is much slower now. She is fourteen but age arrived quickly. At the beginning of the year we walked for miles finding new paths

104

along the coast and I admired the way she followed breathlessly, scrambling over stiles and walls after the others. Now I fear this might have tired her out.

These days I limit her to short expeditions, supposedly after rabbits, and sometimes she does find a burrow and emerges covered with earth as brown as a mole but satisfied. She still responds if she scents a rabbit and her limbs briefly forget their age. On the way back she climbs clumsily into a cow's water-trough; she has always possessed an extraordinary thirst. Whenever she has wanted a drink in my bedroom and I refill the bowl with fresh, cool water, she has made a point of looking up with a 'thank you' nod before she drinks.

Her days are numbered.

'She's all right in herself', said the vet reassuringly when he brought her back this last time. I was tempted to reply: 'But there's not much of *herself* left.'

He admitted there are other growths forming inside her but thinks she will be all right for nine months or so.

'I suppose the point will come,' I asked, 'when we won't be able to cut any more?' He nodded. Meanwhile she relishes life in her amiable way. She is an undemanding dog, her good temper an antidote to Blacky's dourness even though they are sisters. Littlewood was her mother but there are three generations left: Bassey's daughter Alice, and young Bonzo whose black coat is so black and eyes so bright compared to her grandmother's threadbare, almost punch-drunk appearance.

Although she has led a blameless life, Bassey is wearing her age with the jauntiness of a roué. She is becoming pleasantly eccentric having developed a voracious appetite, as well as thirst, with a special weakness for wooden spoons that have stirred a cheese sauce. She found one in the kitchen last night, as the dogs were being locked up, and carried it in her mouth so proudly that I felt guilty at removing it.

She is a tea addict. At night, when she is simply pleased with life or, more likely, thinks she might cadge some dregs of tea at the bottom of the cup, she thumps her tail so loudly on the floor that I have to call out: 'Stop it Bassey! *Stop being so happy!'*

Of course she does get the dregs, and looks up with a lop-sided grin of thanks.

Someone has stated that dogs do not smile. The man who said that can never have smiled himself.

Have you noticed, dogs have been getting the wrong end of the stick recently? If a single guard dog attacks someone there are reports of guard dogs running wild all over the country.

An obscure eye disease is traced to dogs, and television — which is rapidly turning us into a nation of hypochondriacs — gives grave warning, though most opticians in this country have never heard of such a condition.

Above all, there is an outcry against dog pollution in the cities, though this is a natural consequence of life compared to the artificial outpourings of poisoned waste into our rivers and coasts. This campaign started in June 1974 when Bryan Silcock, the Science Correspondent of the *Sunday Times,* announced the startling statistic that dogs deposit 'on our footpaths and open spaces 600 tons of faeces and a million gallons of urine daily'. Such neat sums! How do you measure a million gallons of dog urine in the wide 'open spaces'?

He went on to blame dogs for traffic accidents; for the infection of 'an unknown number' of human beings with 'assorted diseases' (which makes them sound like chocolates), but failed to add that it is easier to catch a disease from your closest friend; finally, he begrudged them the food they eat — 'around 100 000 tons of the most precious of all food resources, animal protein'. Sounds fair enough to me.

Too many dogs, he concludes, and probably he is right as far as unwanted puppies are concerned, but it will be a mean day if some legislation is passed which restricts or exterminates them.

We seem obsessed by such petty legislation these days, and the attempt to reduce all the risk from life which would only lose its flavour too. How typical that the bogey of rabies should have reached such proportions because we are scared for *ourselves.* It would be a tragedy if the disease infected our wild-life and spread through the countryside, but *we* have less chance of being killed by a rabid dog than stung to death by a bumble-bee. In July 1976, the Director-General of the Government-sponsored Health Education Council joined in the campaign by condemning the dog as 'a grubby bag of fur, full to the brim with germs.' Funny that: I have heard of beautiful mongrels but never a beautiful Director-General! An expert warns parents not to allow their children to cuddle their pets — so one of the most innocent joys of growing up is sullied. An M.P. recommends that all dogs be barred from our beaches. We are placing life out of perspective.

106

Also, it is a false argument. Dogs may cause traffic accidents, but if you are blaming the dog you might as well suggest that cars be taken off the roads as well.

The 'anti-dog league' talk of dogs as if they were an unnecessary evil. They forget their generous companionship. When Bernard Levin threw in his weight with his column in *The Times* on 4th November, 1975, *Beware of the Dog,* in which he extolled the superior intelligence of the cat, David McGill wrote to the editor and pointed out nicely that he 'ought to have strengthened his argument by mentioning guide cats for the blind, guardcats, sheepcats, police cats, gun cats, drug sniffing cats, explosive sniffing cats, avalanche rescue cats, even the cat teams in the Arctic.' And asked if Mr Levin was 'merely being "catty"?'

More seriously, R. D. Ryder, a Senior Psychologist at Oxford and member of the RSPCA National Council, replied to Bryan Silcock: 'I often encounter those who overcome loneliness, break down the barriers of shyness, banish depression and despair through sharing their lives with an animal companion.'

To blame the dog is a sign of our own weakness. Cats are notoriously fickle, and human beings treacherous, but the dog is faithful unto death.

The faithful Gelert

The most famous wolfhound in history is the legendary Gelert, given to Llewelyn the Great by King John in 1205. Returning to his castle one night, he found Gelert covered in blood at the nursery door, the bed overturned and his son missing. In rage he thrust his sword through the animal only to discover the child, still alive, though close to the corpse of an immense wolf that had been killed by the faithful Gelert.

The Hon. Robert Spencer (1769–1834) recorded Gelert's death in verse:

> His suppliant looks, as prone he fell,
> No pity could impart;
> But still his Gelert's dying yell
> Passed heavy on his heart.
>
> Arous'd by Gelert's dying yell,
> Some slumb'rer waken'd nigh:
> What words the parent's joy could tell,
> To hear his infant's cry?
>
> Nor scathe had he, nor harm, nor dread:
> But the same couch beneath,
> Lay a gaunt wolf all torn and dead,
> Tremendous still in death.
>
> Ah! what was then Llewelyn's pain?
> For now the truth was clear;
> His gallant hound the wolf had slain
> To save Llewelyn's heir.

Edward Jesse records: 'In order to mitigate his offence (presumably he means 'expiate') Llewelyn built this chapel, and raised a tomb to poor Gelert, and the spot to this day is called *Beth Gelert,* or the Grave of Gelert.' (Today the place is called Beddgelert).

But when I described Gelert as 'legendary', I wrote the literal and deflating truth. Probably such an incident took place somewhere, sometime; it is part of folklore all over the world. But Gelert was the invention of a shrewd publican with a flair for publicity and a desire for profit. He was exposed by D. E. Jenkins in his book *Bedd Gelert: Its Facts, Fairies and Folklore,* published in 1899. Apparently David Pritchard arrived at the village in 1793

108

as the new landlord of the Royal Goat Hotel, and started to think of an enterprise or scheme which would attract customers. The name of the village did mean 'grave of Gelert' and he remembered the Welsh saying 'I repent as much as the man who slew his greyhound'. This was the inspiration he needed! With the connivance of the Parish Clerk, Pritchard erected a gravestone on an appropriate spot and started to spread the story. Finally it reached Spencer who wrote his verses in 1800. All pure invention — and, of course, the tourists flocked.

A Crown of life

HENRY WILLIAMSON
(1895–)

Few men have written about animals with such perception as Henry Williamson. For many years he lived a few miles away from me, at Ox's Cross, above the village of Georgeham which he describes as 'Ham' in *Tales of a Devon Village*. Much of his writing concerns this countryside in North Devon: 'The Old Stag, and other Hunting Stories' set on Exmoor; and his classic, *Tarka the Otter,* which describes the estuary where the Rivers Taw and Torridge rush out to sea and clash at Bideford Bar. We picnicked there, under the remains of the old lighthouse, in the hot early summer of 1975.

This is the landscape for his *Tales of Moorland & Estuary* from which 'A Crown of Life' is taken. There is a humorous dog story too, 'The Dog who ate his Punishment', but 'A Crown of Life' has a quality which is so incomparable that it stands on its own as the closing story in this book. It possesses that savage strength which places Henry Williamson apart. He signed it for me shortly before his eightieth birthday, which was celebrated on 1st December 1975: 'There was my belief — ended — but still alive. Henry Williamson, Georgeham.'

The story starts with an account of the hardness of life in a West Country farmhouse:

> For five centuries the walls and the downstairs floors were damp and the rooms were dark. The yeoman Kiffts worked hard from before sunrise to after sunset during the four seasons; they possessed the lives of their sons, who worked, often beyond middle age, without pay, for their fathers; they shouted at and kicked their ferocious barking cattle dogs as a matter of course; they thought nothing of beating, with their brass buckled belts, their unmarried daughters if they stayed out late without permission; they went regularly to church on Sundays; and they died of rheumatism usually before the age of seventy. A small stream ran beside the wall, just below part of the kitchen floor, giving the place its name of Frogstreet.

Henry Williamson goes on to describe the 'querulous and moody' Clibbit Kifft who inherits the mortaged property and whose fortunes steadily deteriorate, along with his temper. Finally, the misery of such an existence, and his cruelty to all around him, drive his family away. We take up the story as he says goodbye to his wife and baby. The dog stays with him.

''Tes proper, 'tes right, vor you to go away. I ban't no gude. You go away, li'l Clibbit, and don't trouble nought about I. Go along, missus, your carriage be waiting, midear.' Blinking the tears from her eyes, the woman went downstairs with the baby, and out of the

110

house, and Clibbit was left alone with his pony, his dog, a pig, and two cows.

That night he spent in the inn, smiling and nodding his head and praising his wife in a voice that after four glasses of whisky became soft under its perpetual roughness. The neighbours remained silent. Clibbit told them what a beautiful animal was Ship, the grey long-haired sheepdog that followed him everywhere. 'A master dog, aiy!' Ship's head was patted; her tail trembled with gratitude on the stone floor. They said nothing to that, thinking that in the morning the dog's ribs were likely to be broken by one of Oodmall's boots. Ship had long ceased to howl when kicked or beaten by her master. Her eyes flinched white, she crouched from the blow, her eyes closed, and a sort of subdued whimper came from her throat. She never growled nor snarled at Clibbet. Nor did she growl at anything; she seemed to have none of the ordinary canine prejudices or rivalries. Ship was old then. She was a grey shadow slipping in and out of the farmyard doors with Clibbit, or lying in the lane outside, waiting to fetch the cows for milking and returning behind them afterwards. Strangers visiting the village in summer, and pausing to pat the old dog, were likely to wonder why there were so many bumps on her ribs; explanation of the broken ribs was always readily forthcoming from the neighbours.

That evening Clibbit was drunk, but not so happy that he could not find his way down the lane to Frogstreet. He sang in the kitchen, and danced a sort of jig on the slate floor; the first time he had danced and sung since his courting days. In the morning he awoke and got up before daybreak, lit the fire, boiled himself a cup of tea, and ate some bread, cheese, and onions. He milked and fed the two cows himself, watered and fed the pony, and gave the pig its barley meal. Afterwards he and Ship followed behind the cows to the rough pasture in the marshy field called Lovering's Mash; all day he plowed with a borrowed pair of horses, and towards dusk of the wintry day he and Ship brought the cows back to be milked and stalled for the night.

After more bread and cheese, he went up to the inn, drank some whisky, and then smiles broke out of his angular, tufted face and to the neighbours he began to praise wife, li'l ol' pony, dog, and parson. When he had gone home the neighbours said he was a hypocrite.

Clibbit's lonely farming became the joke of the village. He was seen pouring away pails of sour milk into the stream which ran beside Frogstreet and through the garden. He tried to get a woman to look after the dairy, but no one would offer. A letter written by an anonymous neighbour brought the sanitary inspector to Frogstreet; one of the cows was found to be tubercular and ordered to be destroyed. Clibbit sold the other cow to a butcher. He sold his sow to the same butcher a month later. His fields were overgrown with docks, thistles, and sheep's sorrel. His plow stood in one field halfway down a furrow, its rusty share being bound by stroyle grass whose roots it had been cutting when the neighbour had come up and taken away the pair of horses. This neighbour, a hard-working chapel worshipper, intended to buy Frogstreet farm when it came into the market, as inevitably it must. He was the writer of the anonymous letter to the sanitary inspector, and saw to it that everyone knew the property was worth very little; meanwhile he waited to buy it. Clibbit still worked at his traps, always accompanied by old Ship, getting a few shillings a week for rabbits. The neighbours said he didn't eat enough to keep the flesh on a rat.

The pony, already blind from cataract in one eye, and more than twenty years old, developed fever in the feet, and hoping to cure it, for he was fond of it, Clibbit turned it out into Lovering's Mash. It was seen limping about, an inspector came out from town, and Clibbit was summoned to the Court of Summary Jurisdiction.

The stag-hunting chairman of the bench of magistrates, after hearing the evidence of the prosecution, and listening without apparent interest to Clibbit's stammered statement, remarked that he had seen the defendant before him on another occasion. The clerk whispered up to him. H'm, yes. For the callous neglect of the horse, which with the dog was man's best friend — a most un-British line of conduct, he would remark — defendant would be sent to prison for seven days without the option of a fine, and the pony destroyed by Order of the Court. A woman cried, 'Bravo, English justice!' in a shrill triumphant voice; she was turned out of court. The clerk read the next charge, against a terrified and obese individual who had been summoned for riding a bicycle at night without sufficient illumination within the meaning of the Act—to wit, a lamp — who said he had forgotten to light the wick in his haste lest he be late for choir practice. He led the basses, he explained, nervously twisting his hat. Laughter. Clibbit, following a constable through a door, thought the laughter was against him. He had not eaten for three days.

112

That night Ship broke out of the barn, wherein she had been locked, by biting and scratching a way under the rotten doors, and in the morning she was found sitting, whining almost inaudibly, outside the prison gates. The sergeant of police on duty, recognising her, said he would report the stray for destruction, but a young constable, to whom as a small boy Clibbit had once given an apple, said he would look after it until the old Wood Awl came out.

When he came out, his hair cut and his nose not so red, Ship ran round and round him in circles, uttering hysterical noises and trembling violently. Clibbit patted Ship absent-mindedly, as though he did not realise why he or the dog was there, and then set out to walk home.

Next day he was seen about his incult fields, followed by Ship, and mooning about, sometimes stooping to pull a weed — a man with nothing to do.

It was a mild winter, and the frosts had not yet withered the watercress beside the stream running through the small orchard of Frogstreet.

Three weeks before Christmas, Clibbit picked a bunch of watercress and took it to Vellacott farm. 'For the baby,' he said. His brother-in-law told him to take himself off. 'The less us sees of 'ee, the better us'll be plaised,' he said. 'You and your houtrageous cruelty! And I'll tell 'ee this, too, midear: us be puttin' th' law on to 'ee, yesmye, us be suing of 'ee into town, in the court, for to divorce 'ee!'

Clibbit went away without a word. His body was found the next day lying in Lovering's Mash, gun beside him, and Ship wet and whimpering. Watercress was found in his pocket. The coroner's court found a verdict of *felo-de-se,* after much discussion among the jury whether it should be 'suicide while of unsound mind' for the sake of the family.

The neighbours were now sorry for Oodmall, recalling that he had been a 'wonnerful generous chap' sometimes, especially when drunk.

A week before Christmas the ringers began their practice, and the pealing changes of the Treble Hunt fell clanging out of the square Norman tower. It was freezing; smoke rose straight from chimneys. The first to come down the stone steps of the tower and out of the western door, carrying a lantern, were the 'colts', or youths still learning to ring; they saw something flitting grey between the elms which bordered the churchyard and the unconsecrated ground beyond. The colts gave a glance into the darkness; then they hurried down the path, laughing when they were outside the churchyard. But they did not linger there.

Others saw the shadow. The constable, followed and reassured by several men, went among the tombstones cautiously, flashing an electric torch on a heap of earth, still showing shovel marks, without flower or cross — grave of the suicide.

Frogstreet was dark and still, save for the everlasting murmur of flowing water; people hurried past it; and at midnight, when stars glittering were the only light in the valley, the greyness flitted across the yard and stopped, lifting up its head, and a long mournful cry rose into the night.

Towards dawn the cry rose again, as though from the base of the elms; and when daylight came the mound of earth was white with rime, and the long withered grasses were white also, except in one place beside the mound where they were pressed down and green.

The church choir, grouped forms and shadows and a bright new petrol-vapour lamp, went round the village, singing carols. Snow was falling when they walked laughing by the door and blank windows of Frogstreet, on the walls of which their shadows slanted and swerved. The girls laughed shrilly; Christmas was coming and life seemed full and good. Above the wall of the churchyard, raised high by the nameless dead of olden time, two red points glowed steadily. A girl ceased laughing, and put hand to mouth to stop a cry. In the light of the upheld lamp the red points shifted and changed to a soft lambency, and they saw the face of Ship looking down at them. 'Oh, poor thing!' said the girl. She was kitchenmaid at the rectory. The cook told the rector.

The rector was an old man with a white beard, a soft and clear voice, and eyes that had often been very sad when he was young, but now were serene and sure. He had no enemies; he was the friend of all.

Late that night he went to the ground left unconsecrated by ecclesiastical law westwards of the elms and stood by the mound, listening to the sounds of the stream and feeling himself one with the trees and the grass and the life of the earth. This was his prayer; and while he prayed, so still within himself, he felt something warm gently touch his hand, and there, in silence, stood Ship beside him.

The dog followed him to the rectory, and touching the man's

114

hand with its nose, returned to its vigil.

Every morning the rector arose with the sun and went into the churchyard and found Ship waiting for him, and his gift of a biscuit carried in his pocket. Then he entered the church and knelt before the altar, and was still within himself for the cure of souls.

On Christmas Eve the yews in the churchyard were black and motionless as dead Time. The ringers going up the path to the western door saw between the elms a glint and shuffle of light — the rays of their lantern in the icicles hanging from the coat of the dog.

And on Christmas morning the people went into the church while the sun was yet unrisen behind their fields, and knelt in their pews and were still within themselves while the rector's words and the spoken responses were outside the pure aloneness of each one.

With subdued quietness a few began to move down the aisle towards the chancel to kneel by the altar rail behind which the priest waited to minister to them. He moved towards them with the silver paten of bread fragments.

'Take and eat this in remembrance . . .' he was saying, when those remaining in the pews began to notice a small chiming and clinking in the air about them, and as they looked up in wonderment, the movement of other heads drew sight to the figure of the old grey sheepdog walking up the aisle. With consternation they watched it moving slowly towards the light beginning to shine in the stained glass of the tall eastern windows above the altar. They watched it pause before the chancel step, as it stood, slightly swaying, as though summoning its last strength to raise one foot, and a second foot, and again one more foot, and then the last foot, and limp to the row of kneeling people beyond which the rector moved, murmuring the words spoken in olden time by the Friendless One who saw all life with clarity.

The verger hurried on tiptoe across the chancel, but at the look in the rector's eyes, and the slow movement of his head, he hesitated, then returned down the aisle again.

The dog's paw was raised to the rail as it sat there, with dim eyes, waiting; and at every laboured breath the icicles on its coat made their small chimmering noises.

When the last kneeling figure had returned to the pews, with the carved symbols of Crucifixion mutilated in Cromwell's time for

115

religion's sake, the rector bent down beside the dog. They saw him take something from his pocket and hold it out to the dog; then they saw his expression change to one of concern as he knelt down to stroke the head which had slowly leaned sideways as sight unfocused from the dying eyes. They heard the voice saying, slowly and clearly, 'Be thou faithful unto death; and I will give thee a crown of life', and to their eyes came tears, with a strange gladness within their hearts. The sun rose up over the moor, and shone through the eastern windows, where Christ the Sower was radiant.

Tail piece

And so I take leave of you, and walk with the company of my dogs in the fields above.

It is an exhilarating walk. In one field, they catch the scent of an elderly hare, mazing the ground in excitement. They flush it and are off! Their yelps grow fainter as I glimpse them in the distance on the skyline close to Pickwell Manor. Though she is the oldest, Pencil, half whippet, is first in the line of pursuit, with Streaker a breath behind her. Finally they come back and slump on the corn stubble, panting proudly, unsuccessful but satisfied. I like to think that the old hare has enjoyed the excursion too. They have as much chance of catching him as they do the seagulls which they chase on the walk back across the sands, running into the surf, barking frantically as the gulls fly calmly overhead, leading them on.

Occasionally they catch a rabbit, but without the help of gun or snare; a thousand get away.

The sky is darkening. We reach our house again: tongues unfurled, tails aloft as they come down the path.

The walk could never have the same elation without them. Their joy is my contentment.